MY FRIEND SLAPPY

GOOSEBUMPS® HALL OF HORRORS

#1 CLAWS!
#2 NIGHT OF THE GIANT EVERYTHING
#3 SPECIAL EDITION: THE FIVE MASKS OF DR. SCREEM
#4 WHY I QUIT ZOMBIE SCHOOL
#5 DON'T SCREAM!
#6 THE BIRTHDAY PARTY OF NO RETURN

GOOSEBUMPS® MOST WANTED

#1 PLANET OF THE LAWN GNOMES
#2 SON OF SLAPPY
#3 HOW I MET MY MONSTER
#4 FRANKENSTEIN'S DOG
#5 DR. MANIAC WILL SEE YOU NOW
#6 CREATURE TEACHER: FINAL EXAM
#7 A NIGHTMARE ON CLOWN STREET
#8 NIGHT OF THE PUPPET PEOPLE
#9 HERE COMES THE SHAGGEDY
#10 THE LIZARD OF OZ

SPECIAL EDITION #1 ZOMBIE HALLOWEEN
SPECIAL EDITION #2 THE 12 SCREAMS OF CHRISTMAS
SPECIAL EDITION #3 TRICK OR TRAP
SPECIAL EDITION #4 THE HAUNTER

GOOSEBUMPS® SLAPPYWORLD

#1 SLAPPY BIRTHDAY TO YOU
#2 ATTACK OF THE JACK!
#3 I AM SLAPPY'S EVIL TWIN
#4 PLEASE DO NOT FEED THE WEIRDO
#5 ESCAPE FROM SHUDDER MANSION
#6 THE GHOST OF SLAPPY
#7 IT'S ALIVE! IT'S ALIVE!
#8 THE DUMMY MEETS THE MUMMY!
#9: REVENGE OF THE INVISIBLE BOY
#10: DIARY OF A DUMMY
#11: THEY CALL ME THE NIGHT HOWLER!

GOOSEBUMPS®

Also available as ebooks

NIGHT OF THE LIVING DUMMY
DEEP TROUBLE
MONSTER BLOOD
THE HAUNTED MASK
ONE DAY AT HORRORLAND
THE CURSE OF THE MUMMY'S TOMB
BE CAREFUL WHAT YOU WISH FOR
SAY CHEESE AND DIE!
THE HORROR AT CAMP JELLYJAM
HOW I GOT MY SHRUNKEN HEAD
THE WEREWOLF OF FEVER SWAMP
A NIGHT IN TERROR TOWER
WELCOME TO DEAD HOUSE
WELCOME TO CAMP NIGHTMARE
GHOST BEACH
THE SCARECROW WALKS AT MIDNIGHT
YOU CAN'T SCARE ME!
RETURN OF THE MUMMY
REVENGE OF THE LAWN GNOMES
PHANTOM OF THE AUDITORIUM
VAMPIRE BREATH
STAY OUT OF THE BASEMENT
A SHOCKER ON SHOCK STREET
LET'S GET INVISIBLE!
NIGHT OF THE LIVING DUMMY 2
NIGHT OF THE LIVING DUMMY 3
THE ABOMINABLE SNOWMAN OF PASADENA
THE BLOB THAT ATE EVERYONE
THE GHOST NEXT DOOR
THE HAUNTED CAR
ATTACK OF THE GRAVEYARD GHOULS
PLEASE DON'T FEED THE VAMPIRE
THE HEADLESS GHOST
THE HAUNTED MASK 2
BRIDE OF THE LIVING DUMMY
ATTACK OF THE JACK-O'-LANTERNS

ALSO AVAILABLE:

IT CAME FROM OHIO!: MY LIFE AS A WRITER by R.L. Stine

MY FRIEND SLAPPY

R.L. STINE

SCHOLASTIC INC.

Goosebumps book series created by Parachute Press, Inc.

ISBN 978-1-338-35577-2

10 9 8 7 6 5 4 3 2 20 21 22 23 24

Printed in the U.S.A. 40
First printing 2020

SLAPPY HERE, EVERYONE

Welcome to My World.

Yes, it's *SlappyWorld*—you're only *screaming* in it! Hahaha.

I know why you opened this book. You want to get to know me better—don't you!

Is it my good looks or my amazing brain?

Everyone knows I'm so bright, I have to wear sunglasses whenever I look in the mirror!

I'm so quick, I beat myself to the breakfast table! Hahaha!

And take it from me, my beauty isn't skin-deep. That's because I don't have any skin! Hahaha!

People ask why I'm always smiling. It's not because my smile is painted on. It's because I'm so happy to know *me*! Haha.

Everyone wants to be my friend. I can be a good friend—if you don't mind obeying my every command!

Here's a story about a boy named Barton Suggs. He had a lot of problems until I came along. And then, he had a lot of BIG problems! Hahaha.

Barton said he'd do anything to be my friend. Maybe he shouldn't have said that. Barton's wish turns into a very scary story.

I call the story *My Friend Slappy.* I'll let my "friend" Barton tell you all about it.

It's just one more terrifying tale from *SlappyWorld.*

1

I was standing in line to get onto the bus. Someone bumped me hard from behind, and I stumbled into my friend Lizzie Hellman. "Ow!" Lizzie cried out in surprise. And when we stopped stumbling, we both spun around.

Travis Fox had a big grin on his face. It was an ugly grin, the only kind Travis ever has.

I decided to ignore it. Travis was on my case nearly every day, so I was used to it.

My name is Barton Suggs. But Travis and his buddy Kelly Washington call me *Sluggs*, which they think is a riot. They also think it's a riot to shove me into Lizzie.

Dumb, right?

Well, we sixth graders were all lined up to climb onto the school bus in front of our school, Atlantic City Middle School. That's because we were going on a field trip to the famous taffy factory across town. This is the factory where they make DaffyTaffy, which is popular all over the world.

At least, according to my dad. Dad owns the factory.

So okay, I was a little tense about it. I mean, my dad is a good guy, but he can be embarrassing sometimes. Especially when he talks about taffy.

Our teacher, Mr. Plame, was waving us forward. I started onto the bus steps—and tripped. "Whoa!"

Lizzie turned around and grabbed my arm to keep me from falling.

"Hey, Sluggs—walk much?" I heard Travis shout. Then I heard a bunch of kids laughing. I could feel myself blushing.

"It's *Suggs*—not Sluggs!" Lizzie shouted. She led the way to a seat. "Maybe you need glasses," she said to me.

"I don't need glasses," I said. "I'm just a klutz. Did you forget?"

We slid into a seat halfway to the back. Lizzie sat by the window and tossed her long black ponytail behind her shoulder. "Are you excited about going to your dad's factory?" she asked.

I shook my head. "Not really. Dad takes me there a lot. You know, school classes go there all the time. Dad really likes to show it off."

"And everyone gets free taffy?" Lizzie said.

"Yes." I sighed. "I can't even eat taffy. It sticks to my braces."

I turned to the front to see how many kids still had to get on. I saw Travis coming—too late.

He moved toward our seat. Pretended to fall. And landed as hard as he could on his back in my lap.

We both let out screams. Pain shot up my entire body.

Travis is big and wide and heavy. Biggest kid in the class. When he lands on you, you *feel* it!

He has curly blond hair and blue eyes and an angelic round baby face. To look at him, you'd never guess his true personality.

"Oops. Sorry, Sluggs. Guess I slipped." He dug his elbows into my belly.

"Get up! You're crushing me." I groaned.

That made him laugh. He made himself even heavier. I tried to shove him away, but he was too big.

"Travis," Lizzie said, "why are you always so horrible to Barton?"

"Because he's here?"

Travis's friend Kelly appeared and tugged him to his feet. I tried to ignore the pain in my ribs.

"Here's a birthday present for you, Sluggs," Kelly said.

"It's not my birthday," I told him.

"I know," Kelly said. His grin was as ugly as Travis's.

He pulled a huge wet glob of green bubblegum from his mouth and pressed it into the top of my baseball cap.

Then Travis and Kelly stomped to the back of the bus, cackling and bumping knuckles.

So, I guess you can see, those two guys are bad news. They make my life pretty unbearable.

But believe it or not, that was the best part of my day.

A light rain pattered the school bus windows as we rumbled across town. I could see patches of blue sky in the distance. The rain wasn't going to last long.

I gazed toward the front of the bus, thinking hard. I have a supercharged imagination, and I spend a lot of time thinking about horrible things that could happen to Travis and Kelly.

I'm really into puppets and marionettes. I have a pretty big collection. And sometimes I act out scenes with my puppets where these two guys get slapped silly by wooden puppet hands.

I know it's weird. What can I say? Sometimes it makes me feel better.

Lizzie tightened her ponytail, then turned to me. "Travis and Kelly are just jealous of you, Barton," she said.

"Huh? Jealous?"

She nodded. "Because you're so smart, and you get all A's without even trying."

I thought about that for two seconds. I knew Lizzie was wrong. "I don't think they're jealous," I said. "But thanks for thinking that."

Lizzie and I have been good friends ever since fourth grade. I guess we became friends after we accidentally spilled our aquarium science project all over the gym floor and we both got F's.

Yes, she's as klutzy as I am, but she doesn't realize it.

The bus pulled into the industrial park where my dad's factory is. We slowed to a stop at the front of the parking lot.

Mr. Plame jumped up from his seat. He is way tall, and he bumped his head on the bus ceiling. "One at a time as you get off the bus, people," he said, rubbing his head. "Best behavior, remember?"

I hoped Travis and Kelly heard that.

Mr. Plame stepped down to the ground, and we started to pile off the bus. Some kids behind me started a chant: "*Daffy! Taffy! Daffy! Taffy!*" But it didn't last long.

The rain had stopped. The air was warm and wet.

I followed Lizzie off the bus. And there came my dad, bursting out from the glass front doors and hurrying over to greet us.

My dad never walks. He was a football fullback in college, and he still thinks he's charging the line, moving faster than everyone else.

He's big and brawny, like a fullback. He always

looks ready to spring forward, even when he's standing still. And he almost never stays still. Mom says she has to tie him to the chair to keep him at the dinner table for a whole meal.

You can guess that I don't take after him. How would I describe myself? A little more timid, maybe. I'm definitely not an athlete like he was. The sad truth is, no one chooses me for any sports teams ever.

Dad wore a pink-and-yellow DaffyTaffy cap. And a white work shirt and pants, even though he doesn't do any factory work.

"Welcome, everyone," Dad boomed when we were all off the bus. He never talks. He always booms. "Welcome to the largest and best taffy factory in the universe!"

That embarrassed me a little bit. Why did he have to brag like that?

Mr. Plame shook hands with my dad. Then he turned to me. "You're lucky, Barton," he said. "You probably get more taffy to eat than any kid in the world."

"Not really," I murmured. I didn't want to say that I can't eat taffy for at least another year, till my braces come off.

"This way, everyone!" Dad boomed, waving to the entrance. "I'm going to give you the tour myself. I think you'll learn a lot about taffy!"

We started to the entrance. Kelly stomped on my foot as he hurried past me.

I limped after him, holding my breath, waiting for the pain in my foot to fade.

My dad stood at the door, greeting each kid as they entered the factory.

I said hi as I stepped up to him.

"Hey, Barton," he said. "You—"

He stopped. His smile faded.

He put both hands on my shoulders and pulled me aside.

"We have to talk."

My dad pulled me into the building and down a short hall. The air smelled sweet. The taffy was cooking at the back of the factory, but I could smell it all the way up here.

Dad narrowed his eyes at me. “You have a problem, Barton.”

“Huh? What’s the matter?”

He lifted the cap off my head and held it in front of me. “You have a big glob of green gunk on the top of your cap.”

“I know,” I said.

He stared hard at the gum on my cap. “Is this something kids are doing these days? To be cool?”

“Not really,” I said.

Down the hall, the kids from my class waited with Mr. Plame. A lot of them were watching Dad and me. I knew they were wondering what was up. I caught a glimpse of Lizzie leaning against the wall. She looked very worried.

Dad studied the cap some more. He pulled the

gum off and wrapped it up in a tissue. Then he handed it back to me. "Was it those two bullies again?" he demanded.

I sighed.

A few weeks ago, I made the mistake of telling him about Travis and Kelly. I was having a really bad day, and it all just slipped out. Of course, I was sorry I told him as soon as it happened because Dad said he was going to go to their houses and talk to their parents about it.

Yikes.

How embarrassing would that be? Not to mention life-threatening. If my dad did that . . . If he squealed to their parents . . . Travis and Kelly would probably *kill* me!

But that's what Dad is like. He was a fast-charging fullback in school, and he's a fast-charging fullback in life.

I begged him and begged him not to talk to their parents. I actually got down on my knees, and finally Dad gave in.

But after that, he kept talking about it all the time. He kept urging me to stand up to them.

Easy to say when you've never been bullied, right?

He gave me one last tsk-tsk. Then he spun away from me and hurried to the others. He motioned for everyone to follow him, and he led us into the factory.

As soon as he opened the door, the aroma of

the heated sugar floated over us. So sweet. At first, it was actually hard to breathe.

More than a dozen workers in white uniforms were tending to the huge machines scattered over the factory floor. They didn't look up when we entered. They were used to Dad leading school groups through the place.

My class followed Dad up to the machine that stretched the taffy. It looked like a tall robot with very long arms. The taffy was draped over the arms. The arms kept moving in and out, pulling the taffy.

"We stretch over two tons of taffy a year!" Dad boasted. "Those arms are strong. They can stretch a hundred pounds of taffy at a time."

Dad stepped away so everyone could watch the taffy-stretching machine. Kelly edged up to me—and bumped me hard with his shoulder. "Oops. Sorry."

I stumbled sideways and nearly knocked Dad over. He turned and stared at Kelly.

"Is that the boy who stuck gum on your cap?" Dad asked in a whisper. "Is that him?"

"Well . . ."

"Go ahead. Stand up to him," Dad said. He took my shoulders and turned me around so I was facing Kelly.

My heart started to pound. I had a fluttery feeling in my chest.

I didn't want to do it. No way. I'm not a fighter.

But Dad was watching me.

I took three quick strides and stepped up behind Kelly. I wrapped my arms around his waist—and hoisted him off the floor.

He made a choking sound. He was too surprised to cry out.

And he had no time to struggle.

I lifted him high—and *heaved* him into the taffy stretcher.

Some kids cried out as the taffy wrapped around Kelly. And then the robot arms moved out, pulling him one way. They moved in, pushing him the other way.

"He's being *stretched!*" I heard someone scream.

And then Kelly began to wail: "Help me! It's stretching me! I can't breathe! Owwwww! It's stretching me!"

4

Of course, I didn't *really* pick Kelly up and heave him into the taffy machine.

I only imagined it.

I told you, I have a wild imagination. Sometimes what I dream up seems totally real to me. Do you think that's weird?

Well, I wished this fantasy was real. But no way. No way I could ever do that to anyone.

Instead, I just gave Kelly my angriest stare. I don't think he even noticed.

Once again, I pictured Kelly tangled in the taffy, screaming his head off in front of the whole class.

"Barton, why are you smiling?" Lizzie asked.

"Just thinking about something," I said. "Do you ever think about getting revenge against people?"

Before Lizzie could answer, Mr. Plame called across the room. "Lizzie? Barton? What's up with you two?"

"Uh . . . just talking about taffy," I said.

Some kids laughed. I heard Travis and Kelly whispering about us.

"Now, everyone follow me," Dad boomed. He pointed up to the high ceiling. "We're going to climb up to that catwalk so you can all get a good view of the flavor vats."

He started to climb a ladder that led up to the catwalk. "I need you all to stay in a single line," Dad continued. "And hold on to the railing. The catwalk is sturdy. But it's very high up."

He stepped onto the long, narrow catwalk and turned back to the class. "Wish I had better insurance! Haha!"

It was supposed to be a joke, but no one really got it, so no one laughed.

Dad backed along the catwalk as we all climbed up. "Taffy was invented right here in Atlantic City," he said. "Sometime in the late nineteenth century."

I rolled my eyes. I'd heard Dad's taffy lecture a hundred times. He even gave it sometimes at dinner.

I was at the top of the ladder. Lizzie turned and helped pull me onto the catwalk. It was like a long, narrow wooden bridge. It stretched high above the factory floor.

"We make saltwater taffy here," Dad continued. "How did taffy get salty? Well, there's a story behind it. A man named David Bradley had a candy store here in Atlantic City. And in 1883, there was a massive flood. And all of his taffy was soaked with salt water from the Atlantic Ocean."

Dad stopped to clear his throat. "But Bradley got lucky. Because people tasted it and they *liked* the salty candy. So the recipe changed—and now we make taffy with salt."

I don't really like heights. I held on to the rail and peered down to the floor below. We were standing over enormous open vats. One vat was filled nearly to the top with a pink liquid. The one right beneath Lizzy and me was dark brown.

"You're looking at our flavor vats," Dad said. "The one directly beneath you is pure chocolate. We are very proud that our cocoa beans are the highest quality. They come all the way from Brazil."

He turned to the class. "Doesn't that smell *amazing*?"

Most everyone agreed.

"This has to be the biggest cup of hot chocolate in the world!" Dad declared. He motioned toward the far end of the catwalk. "Let's move on."

I took a few steps—and uttered a cry when I felt a hard bump from behind.

Was it Travis or Kelly? Or just someone who accidentally bumped into me?

No time to think about it.

The bump sent me stumbling forward. My hands slipped off the railing. I couldn't get my balance.

I fell . . . fell forward . . . Toppled over the railing.

Not my imagination. Not a hallucination.

Real. I was really falling. Screaming all the way down.

Headfirst into the hot chocolate.

I landed with a heavy *splaaaash.* And tried to hold my breath as I sank deep into the hot goo.

5

I cut off my scream and shut my eyes as I hit the warm liquid. The fall carried me to the bottom of the vat. The chocolate was thick, like wet cement.

Panic swept over me. I couldn't move. I felt waves of chocolate spinning around me. And then the spinning stopped.

I raised my arms and forced myself to push off from the bottom. My clothes stuck to my body and weighed me down. My chest felt ready to burst.

Thrashing hard, I pulled myself up to the surface. I raised my head over the chocolate and took in breath after breath.

I lifted my hands and tried to wipe the chocolate off my eyes. I heard sirens blaring. Bells were ringing. I heard alarmed shouts all around.

"Ohhh," I moaned as I started to sink into the chocolate again. Panic gripped me, and I froze for a few seconds. Then I started to thrash my arms again, pulling myself up over the hot surface.

I spewed a spray of chocolate up into the air. My chest heaved as I struggled to breathe.

Then I saw arms reaching for me. White-uniformed workers had climbed to the top of the vat. They stretched their hands toward me.

Slapping the thick surface, I pulled myself to the side and grabbed a pair of hands. I felt as if I weighed two hundred pounds. The worker pulled me closer to the side of the vat. Then more hands dragged me up and out.

The sirens kept wailing. Workers were running around frantically. My whole body shuddered and shook. I was covered from head to foot in a thick layer of chocolate.

I was still trying to wipe the goo away from my eyes when Dad came rushing up. "Are you okay? Can you breathe? What happened? How did you fall?" he demanded.

"I . . . I . . ."

I couldn't speak.

Dad shook his head. "We have to throw out the entire batch," he said. "It's ruined. It's a total loss."

"Sorry," I murmured. What else could I say?

I raised my eyes and saw that the class was back down on the factory floor. They were all staring at me. Mr. Plame stood off to the side with Travis and Kelly. The teacher had a stern look on his face.

Both boys were gesturing with their hands and talking at once.

"We didn't touch him. I swear," I heard Travis say.

"We didn't bump him," Kelly said. "He fell on his own. Honest."

"Seriously. I saw him start to fall," Travis told the teacher. "I tried to catch him but I was too late."

"We didn't bump him!"

I turned away and saw Dad pull two workers over. "Get Barton to the showers," Dad ordered. "Hurry. The chocolate is starting to harden. It'll never come off!"

The next day was Saturday. I was so happy I didn't have to go to school and face everyone in my class. I'm sure they'd all have a lot of chocolate jokes for me.

I kept thinking about Travis and Kelly. Did one of them deliberately shove me over the side of the railing? The thought was totally scary.

They were mean kids. But they weren't *that* mean—were they?

Dad went out in the morning. When he came back, he was carrying a large case. It looked like a guitar case.

"Barton, I brought you a present," he said. "I thought it might cheer you up."

He set the case down on the dining room table. "Go ahead. Open it."

I clicked the two clasps on the side of the case and lifted the lid. "Oh, wow," I murmured. I stared down at an old ventriloquist dummy and smiled.

The dummy lay on its back, its arms crossed over its chest. It wore a stained gray suit and a tilted red bow tie over a white shirt. Its lips were painted red, and it grinned right back at me.

"A new puppet for your collection. I thought it might help cheer you up," Dad said. We both leaned over the case, studying the dummy.

"He's weird looking," I said. "See his grin. It's not really a smile. It looks kind of evil."

Dad chuckled. "Barton, with your wild imagination, I'm sure you'll give him a good personality."

I reached into the case and carefully picked up the dummy. His shoes and hands were carved of wood. "He's heavy," I said.

"I think the dummy is pretty old," Dad said. "His name is Slappy."

"Slappy?" I said. "What a lame name."

Dad shrugged. "That's what I was told. He comes with a couple of sheets of instructions. They're tucked into his jacket pocket."

I balanced Slappy on one arm and reached inside his back with my other hand. I found the controls and made his mouth move up and down. *"Hiya, Dad. I'm Slappy. I'm kinda ugly!"* I made the dummy say in a high, squeaky voice.

Dad smiled. "I thought maybe you could work up some kind of act with Slappy," he said. "You know. Like a comedy act you could perform at school or birthday parties or something."

His smile faded. "It could help you be less shy."

There Dad goes again.

He never can drop the subject of how shy I am. He has to keep pushing me . . . pushing me to be more like him. Loud and bold. Not afraid of anything.

He didn't buy this dummy to cheer me up. He gave it to me because he thought it might help make me better.

I felt a flash of anger, but I fought it down. "Hey, thanks, Dad," I said. "I'm sure I can do something with him."

I tossed the dummy over my shoulder and carried him up to my room. I sat him on the windowsill and propped him up against the glass.

I didn't feel like playing with him. I was too depressed. And I still felt achy and weird from my fall into the chocolate vat.

I stepped back and took one last look at the dummy. "Hey, dummy, why did someone decide to make you so ugly?" I said.

Then I gasped.

Did its eyes blink up and down?

No. That didn't happen.

That had to be my crazy imagination again, right?

SLAPPY HERE, EVERYONE

Well . . . finally! An interesting character appears in this story. ME! Hahaha.

Don't call me Slappy. You can just call me Schoolteacher. Because I'm about to teach Barton a few lessons! Haha.

If he thinks *I'm* ugly, wait till he sees what he looks like when I get through with him!

Oooh! It gives me happy shudders just thinking about it!

That afternoon, I was gazing out the front window, watching dark storm clouds move across the sky. Lizzie came into view, walking at the end of the block. She wore a long black rain poncho. The black coat against the gray trees and houses made her look like she was in an old black-and-white movie.

She was halfway along the block when she stopped. Even from this far away, I could see the terrified look on her face. I knew why she was afraid.

Kraken, the Grimm family's huge dog, was charging toward her, barking like a monster. Luckily, Kraken was chained up on a short leash.

Kraken really *is* like a monster. He snarls and growls and dives at everyone who passes by, snapping huge teeth. People in the neighborhood have all complained about how dangerous Kraken is. But the Grimms say they need a good watchdog. And Kraken could never get off his chain.

Ha.

I'm scared every time I walk by him. Lizzie and I almost always cross the street so we can pass the big beast on the other side.

Lizzie is so kind. Once she said she thought Kraken was just lonely. "He's always alone, chained up in the front yard, without anyone to show him any attention," she said.

Maybe she's right. But there's *no way* she and I were brave enough to get close and make friends with him!

Lizzie loves dogs. But her parents won't let her have one because she's allergic. Instead, she has a huge collection of stuffed dogs in her room. There are at least a hundred of them, and every one of them has a name.

Some of her friends think a stuffed dog collection is babyish. But Lizzie doesn't care. She likes her stuffed dogs!

Peering out the window, I saw Kraken charge at Lizzie, snapping his jaws. He's so huge, his paws thunder against the ground when he runs. I could hear the thud of his footsteps through the closed window.

Kraken ran to the end of his chain and nearly choked himself straining against it, howling and growling at Lizzie. When she saw that he couldn't reach her, she took off running.

I watched her race up my driveway, and I pulled

the front door open before she had a chance to ring the bell.

She was breathing hard. She blinked as she stared at me, catching her breath.

And then she let out a loud, shrill scream.

8

"Lizzie—what is it?" I cried.

She took a deep breath and held it. "Oh. Sorry, Barton. Your face—it's so weird. I didn't realize you were burned so badly in the vat of hot chocolate."

I shook my head. "I'm not burned," I said. "I'm allergic to chocolate."

"Oh, wow. Too bad, Barton." She pushed past me into the house. "You really look like a hideous monster."

"Thanks. You're cute, too," I muttered. "Did you come over to cheer me up or what?"

She tossed her rain parka onto the back of a living room chair. "Sorry. Does it hurt? Do you feel bad?"

"Well . . . this red rash broke out all over my body," I said. "And my skin itches and burns everywhere."

Lizzie took a handful of pretzels from the bowl on the coffee table. "Sad," she murmured.

I sighed. "I'll bet the whole class is laughing at me."

She swallowed some pretzels. "Well . . . some kids are calling you *Daffy Taffy*."

"Yaaaaiiii." I wanted to scream. "That's worse than *Sluggs*," I moaned.

Lizzie shrugged. "They'll forget about it . . . someday."

"This is terrible," I said, dropping onto the edge of the couch. "My skin is red and blotchy. The kids are all laughing at me. And my dad is furious because I ruined thousands of dollars' worth of chocolate."

Lizzie took another handful of pretzels. "Barton, let me tell you a story that will cheer you up," she said. "It's about a time when I fell, too."

"You had a bad fall like me?" I said.

She nodded. "I was at a birthday party. In fourth grade. At my old school. And it was at this girl's house. I really wanted to impress her."

"And what happened?" I asked.

"I was walking by the table with her birthday cake on it," Lizzie continued. "And I wasn't watching where I was going because I was staring at a boy I liked across the room. And I tripped and fell over my own shoes."

"Headfirst into the birthday cake?" I said. "You destroyed the birthday cake?"

"Almost," Lizzie said. "I almost fell into the cake, but I just missed it."

My mouth dropped open. "Is that the story? Is that the story that's supposed to cheer me up?"

She nodded.

"Lame!" I cried. "It's totally lame!"

Lizzie lowered her head. "Sorry. I was just trying to help."

I sighed. "You can't help me with a lame story like that. This is serious."

She reached for the pretzel bowl. Changed her mind. Clasped her hands in her lap. "Yes, I know. Barton, do you think Travis and Kelly deliberately pushed you off the catwalk?"

The question made my breath catch in my throat. I shrugged my shoulders. "I don't know. I really can't be sure."

Lizzie didn't say anything. She shut her eyes behind her glasses.

"Is it possible they really wanted to *hurt* me?" I said. "Is it possible they hate me so much . . . that I'm not *safe*?"

"I . . . I don't know," Lizzie stammered.

"I could have drowned in that chocolate, Lizzie," I said, my voice just above a whisper. "I know *someone* pushed me. I'm scared. I really am."

Lizzie went home. From the front window, I watched her walking back to her house. As usual, Kraken went nuts as she came near. The big monster dog pulled so hard on his chain, he nearly strangled himself again.

Lizzie took off and ran across the street just to be safe.

I felt bad. I wasn't very nice to her. She had come over to help cheer me up. And I yelled at her and told her that her falling-down story was lame.

I tried to stop thinking about the class trip. But I couldn't get my mind back to normal. I kept seeing myself flying off the factory catwalk again and again. I felt dizzy just from the memory of that headfirst tumble into the vat. I mean, how could anyone stop thinking about that?

I went upstairs to my room to do my homework. Maybe that would take my mind off things. But I finished all my assignments in just ten minutes.

What can I say? I'm a brainiac!

A lot of good it does me.

I'm a brainiac, and I'm the class joke.

I paced back and forth for a few minutes. My room is long and narrow, so it's good for tromping back and forth. But there's only so long you can do that without getting bored.

I lifted the big case that held the dummy Dad bought me and set it on my bed. I opened the lid and stared down at the grinning dummy. Its glassy green eyes were wide open and seemed to stare back up at me.

I saw a small chip in the paint on its nose. The grinning lips were rose red.

I reached into the pocket of the suit jacket and pulled out two folded-up sheets of paper. Dad said the dummy came with some kind of instructions.

I glanced at the first page. All it said was *Hi. My name is Slappy. Do you want to be my friend?*

I unfolded the other sheet of paper. It had a bunch of words on it in a strange foreign language. I started to read the words out loud: *"Karru Marri Odonna . . ."*

But then I stopped.

I wasn't in the mood to think up a ventriloquist act. I had to wait till I felt in a funnier mood.

I tucked both papers into the dummy's pocket. Then I dropped him onto the bed. I walked to the closet and pulled out my two favorite marionettes.

One of them is a tall, awesome-looking dude in

a khaki soldier's uniform. I call him Bart, after me. I know it's weird, but sometimes I pretend I'm a tough guy like him.

The other puppet is a clown with a round red nose and wild red hair that stands straight up. He wears a baggy blue-and-white-striped costume with a big ruffle around the neck, and he has a dopey grin painted across his face.

I call him Travis.

"Get him, Bart!" I shouted. And I made the soldier puppet attack the clown.

Pound. Pound. Pound.

Bart slapped Travis with his wooden fist. I made Travis fall to his knees.

Pound pound pound.

"No mercy!" I shouted. "No mercy for a clown like you!"

Maybe you think it's babyish. But a good puppet fight always makes me feel better.

"Please don't hit me! Please!" I made the clown whine.

Pound pound pound.

Sure, it wasn't real revenge. But it was the best I could do.

I stood the puppets up and was about to start the fight again—when I heard the front doorbell ring.

Is it Lizzie? I wondered. *Did she come back to try to cheer me up again?*

I draped the marionettes over my bed and ran downstairs to open the front door.

"Oh." I uttered a startled cry when I saw who was standing there.

Travis and Kelly.

10

"Wh-wh-wh—" I tried to speak, but I was too shocked.

Travis shoved a big chocolate bar into my hands. He grinned. "We thought you might like this."

Ha ha. Very funny.

What do they want?

What are they going to do to me now?

Kelly squinted at me. "What are those sores on your face?" he demanded.

"It's a rash. From the fall," I said.

"Looks good on you!" Kelly said. Laughing, they slapped knuckles.

"Good-bye," I said. I started to slam the door shut. But Travis blocked it with his wide body.

"We want to talk to you," he said.

"We have a deal for you, Barton," Kelly added.

Barton? He didn't call me Sluggs?

Travis tried to step into the house, but I blocked his way. "What kind of deal?"

"You'll like it," Travis said. "Come on. Let us in. We're not going to hurt you."

I didn't move. "Hurt me? You tried to *kill* me! You pushed me—"

"No way!" they both cried at once.

"I didn't push you. I swear!" Travis said, raising his right hand.

"I didn't do it, either," Kelly said.

I stared at them. Were they telling the truth? I didn't believe them. Somebody bumped me. I didn't just fall.

"Can we come in? We just want to talk," Travis said.

I thought about it for a few seconds. Then I stepped back and let them into the house.

No one was home but me. Was I making a big mistake?

They followed me up to my room.

"Are those puppets?" Kelly asked, pointing to the two I had draped over the bed.

"They're marionettes," I said. "I've been collecting them since I was five. Some of them are valuable."

Kelly picked up the controller for the soldier. He lowered the puppet to the floor and tried to figure out how to make him walk.

Travis snickered. "Hey, are these your *friends*?"

I could feel myself blushing. "It . . . it's just a hobby," I said.

Before I could stop him, Travis picked up the controller for the clown and lowered the puppet to the floor. "The clown ATTACKS!" he cried. He swung the puppet into the soldier.

"Hey, stop—!" I shouted.

Too late. The strings were all tangled.

I grabbed the controllers from them and carried the tangled marionettes to my closet. When I turned around, Travis had picked up Slappy.

"Barton, is this another buddy of yours?"

"Do you talk to him?" Kelly asked, grinning. "Do you tell him all your secrets?"

Travis grabbed the dummy's head and spun it around so it was facing backward. "Haha. Look! He looks better this way!"

"Put it down. Please," I said. "He's very old."

Travis twisted the head around some more.

"I thought you wanted to talk to me," I said, grabbing Slappy away from him. I walked to the window and set him down on the windowsill. "You said you had a deal for me?"

Kelly dropped down onto the edge of my bed. He picked his nose and wiped his finger on my bedspread.

Travis laughed. "That's gross."

I pointed to the door. "You have to go," I said. "I'm serious."

"No. Wait," Travis said. "We have a deal. You'll

like it." He spun my desk chair around and sat down on it.

I stood watching them both, my arms crossed tightly in front of my chest. "What's the deal?"

They exchanged glances. "We'll stop picking on you," Travis said. "We'll stop giving you a hard time."

My mouth dropped open. "Huh? You're joking, right?"

"No joke," Kelly replied. "I swear. We'll stop being mean to you. And we'll stop calling you Sluggs. And we'll stop making you look like a jerk in front of everyone. I swear."

"Why?" I said.

"We're not finished," Travis said. "Give us a chance, Barton."

"You know the Crokodile Tears concert at the civic center?" Kelly said. "You heard about it?"

I nodded.

"It's the hottest ticket in town," he continued. "I mean, it's been sold out for months."

"I know," I said. "Everyone is into Crokodile Tears. They're awesome."

"Well, Travis and I will give you a ticket for the concert," Kelly said.

I stared hard at him. "What kind of joke is this?"

Kelly shook his head. "Not a joke. We'll give you a ticket. Ten rows from the stage."

"And we'll let you hang with us at the concert," Travis chimed in.

"For real?" I still didn't believe them.

"Yes. For real," Travis answered. "It's all real, Barton. You just have to do something for us."

I squinted at him. "What do I have to do?"

11

"It's simple," Travis said.

"Totally easy," Kelly agreed.

"What?" I demanded. "What do I have to do?"

"Write our final book reports," Travis said.

"It's so easy for you, Barton," Kelly said. "The book reports count for half our grade."

"And we haven't even read the books yet," Travis said.

"What books did you choose?" I asked.

They both shook their heads.

"We didn't even choose yet," Travis said. "We're totally behind. You could choose whatever books you want, Barton."

"And write the book reports for us," Kelly said. "Yours is already written, right?"

I nodded. "Of course. It's due on Wednesday."

"Then you have time to write ours," Kelly said. "You'll get an A on yours. You always do. You can just get us B's for ours."

"Yeah. B's would be awesome," Travis agreed.

He raised his eyes to mine. "And if you do it, Kelly and I will be your best friends. We'll be nice to you, Barton."

"We'll be super nice," Kelly said. "You won't believe how nice we'll be. Seriously. We'll be best friends forever."

I blinked a few times. My head felt like it was spinning the way Slappy's head spun. I stared at them. Studied them. Were they serious? Yes. They looked serious.

I started to think about how my life would change. If I wrote their book reports for them, it would all be different. No more torture. No more mean tricks. No more making me feel like a total jerk.

I'd be free. Free of the two bullies who had been ruining every day of my life.

But, whoa. Wait.

I wasn't thinking clearly at all.

This was cheating. The worst kind of cheating. The most dangerous kind of cheating.

It could get all three of us kicked out of school. Even worse, it would go on my permanent record. My crime would follow me for the rest of my life.

If I said yes to this, it could ruin my life forever. I'd be a disgrace. Everyone would know. My parents would be horrified and ashamed of me. They would never let me forget what I had done.

On the other hand . . .

It wouldn't be hard to write two more book reports. Writing comes so easily to me. And I could write them in different styles. Make them sound different from each other. That would be fun.

And think how much better my life would be. How much happier I would be without the two bullies. They'd go from bullies to buddies. We'd be a squad.

I didn't realize my eyes had been shut while I thought about all this. I opened my eyes to see the two guys staring hard at me.

Travis held Slappy in his arms. He made the dummy's mouth move up and down. And in a high, squeaky voice, he made Slappy say: "Well, Barton? What's your answer? Will you do it?"

"No," I said.

12

Their mouths dropped open. Travis tossed Slappy onto the bed.

"Are you sure?" Travis asked. His hands curled into fists at his sides. "You don't want to make the wrong choice, do you?"

Kelly squinted hard at me. His cheeks had angry red circles on them.

They both studied me, standing tense and stiff. Waiting for me to say yes.

"No, I can't do it," I said. My voice came out tiny and shaky.

Kelly shook his head. "Maybe you need some time to think about it, Sluggs," he said. "You might be making a big mistake. Know what I'm saying?"

"A very big mistake," Travis added. He pounded a fist into his other hand.

I got his meaning.

"Things could get tough if you make the wrong choice," Kelly said. His cheeks were still an angry red, almost purple now. His whole body was tensed, as if ready to fight.

A chill ran down my back. My heart was racing in my chest.

Sure, I was scared of these two guys. But I was even more frightened of what would happen to me if I was caught cheating for them.

Travis picked Slappy up from the bed. He twisted the dummy's head again. Then he lowered the dummy in front of him—and kicked it across the room.

Slappy's wooden head bounced twice against the floor. The dummy sprawled all bent and twisted, facedown.

I tried to swallow, but my mouth was dry as cotton.

I'm going to do the right thing, I told myself. *I'm not going to cheat. Even if it puts me in a world of pain.*

The two boys started to the door. "Think it over, Sluggs," Kelly said. He gave Slappy a hard kick in the stomach. The dummy flew up, then flopped down again with a *thud.*

"We're nice guys," Travis said. "We're going to give you a second chance to make the right choice."

I stood there without moving and listened to them clomp down the stairs. The front door slammed behind them.

I let out a long whoosh of air. I didn't realize I'd been holding my breath.

"Barton, you did the right thing," I said out loud.

Or did I?

I lifted the dummy off the floor. I straightened his suit jacket and placed him carefully on his back on the bed. Slappy grinned up at me as if nothing had happened.

As if I hadn't made a decision that would ruin the rest of my life.

I pulled the two marionettes from the closet. Travis and Kelly had tangled their strings and I wanted to untangle them. But my hands were shaking too hard. It would have to wait till later.

I knew what I wanted. I wanted to walk over to Lizzie's house and tell her what Travis and Kelly wanted me to do. I knew Lizzie would back me up. I knew she'd agree that I did the right thing.

I left Mom and Dad a note saying I was going over to Lizzie's. Then I stepped out the front door. I had a sudden shiver of fear. Were Travis and Kelly waiting for me outside the house?

No.

Chill, Barton. You've got to calm down.

I started to walk. The storm clouds had cleared, and the sun was high in a solid blue sky. I raised my face to it and let the warmth spread over me. I suddenly wished I was at the beach, listening to the steady roar of ocean waves.

I love the beach. That's the nice thing about living in Atlantic City. You're never far from the ocean.

I was still thinking about the ocean and the splash of waves when I heard a dog's sharp bark. I snapped out of my daydream. And saw the huge monster dog, Kraken, a few houses ahead.

Snarling, baring his long fangs, Kraken rose up on his hind paws, pulling hard at his chain leash. The links made a snapping sound.

And there were Travis and Kelly. They were down on their knees in the grass. They were huddled over the dog's chain. Working on it. Loosening it! Unhooking it!

Kraken raised his head high and wailed at me.

"Hey, Sluggs—!" Travis shouted over the cry of the dog. "Want to play with the nice doggy?"

I started to run.

Laughing hard, the two boys pulled the chain free. I turned and saw Kraken come roaring at me. Huge paws thundering over the grass. His eyes bulging. His jaws snapping loudly. A huge wad of saliva flew from his open mouth as he came charging toward me.

I was too slow.

Kraken was too fast.

There was no time . . . no time.

I could still hear the two boys laughing as Kraken leaped to attack.

"Ohhhhh." A moan escaped my throat as the big dog rose up in front of me.

I staggered back. Not quick enough.

The paws—as big as baseball gloves—pounded my shoulders.

I smelled his sour breath. It poured hot over my face like steam. The paws shoved hard, and I toppled onto my back.

I landed on the grass with a heavy *thud*. The dog pounced on me, covered me like a smothering fur blanket, hot and heavy.

He snapped his jaws. Sticky saliva spattered my face. The dog dug his teeth into my shirt-sleeve and tore it right and left.

Buried beneath his weight, I struggled to push him off. But he was too heavy. I tried to roll out from under his heaving belly. But he pressed down hard, tearing at my shirt.

He's going to rip my arm off!

Then a wave of panic shot down my body as I felt his sharp, wet teeth wrap around my wrist.

I gasped. Shut my eyes. Waited for the pain.

And then I heard a shrill whistle. Three long bleats.

"Huh?" I uttered a sharp cry as I felt the dog's teeth loosen.

I opened my eyes and saw Kraken backing away. Panting hard, head still lowered, growling, as if ready to return to the attack.

Three more whistle blasts. Like a traffic cop's whistle.

I raised my head. And tried to focus my eyes.

Kraken made whimpering sounds as he turned and slumped back toward the Grimms' house.

I slowly pulled myself to a sitting position. I felt dizzy. My eyes still wouldn't focus. I was gasping for breath. My arm throbbed, but I hadn't been cut.

"Hey, Barton—! Are you okay?"

I turned and saw Mr. Grimm running across the lawn toward me, a silvery whistle bobbing at his neck. Travis and Kelly stood in the driveway, their hands in their jeans pockets.

"Are you okay?" Mr. Grimm stopped and peered down at me.

"I . . . think so," I choked out.

He took my hands and pulled me to my feet. He brushed leaves off the back of my shirt. "No cuts? No broken bones?"

I shook myself and rolled my arm around. "No. I guess I'm okay. Just scared. You know. My heart's still going crazy."

Mr. Grimm turned to Travis and Kelly, who had walked up behind him. "How did the dog get loose?"

Both boys shrugged.

"Beats me," Travis said. "Kelly and I got here at just the right time."

"Yeah," Kelly agreed. "We saw the dog break loose and go running at Barton. We tried to stop Kraken. But we didn't know how."

Liars.

"We were scared, too," Travis said. "We thought the dog would turn and go after *us*!"

Liars. Liars.

They removed the chain and set the monster after me.

And now they're lying about it with totally innocent faces.

I took a deep breath. Then I opened my mouth to tell Mr. Grimm the truth. I wanted Travis and Kelly to be punished. I wanted Mr. Grimm to know what really happened.

Travis and Kelly were still talking, adding to their lies. "I wanted to tackle Kraken," Travis said. "But he was too fast."

"Barton is our friend. We wanted to save him," Kelly said. "But we didn't know if you were home."

Lies, lies, lies.

I took another deep breath. I changed my mind.

What was the point in trying to tell Mr. Grimm the truth?

Telling the truth wouldn't help me at all.

Suddenly, I knew exactly what I had to do.

14

Two nights later, I was sitting on the edge of my bed with Slappy the dummy on my lap. I was practicing moving his mouth and making his eyes slide from side to side.

I knew I was wasting time. Stalling.

I didn't want to do what I knew I had to do.

"What do you think of Travis and Kelly, Slappy?" I asked.

I made the dummy's mouth click up and down. *"Hate them!"* I made Slappy say in a high, tinny voice. *"I think they're dummies!"*

"What should we do when we see them?" I asked.

"I'd rather SEE them than BE them!" I made Slappy say.

"Maybe I *can* work up a funny comedy act with this dummy," I told myself. But not now. I had work to do.

I lay Slappy on his back on the bedspread and crossed the room to my laptop. I fought away the heavy feeling of dread in the pit of my stomach and sat down at the keyboard.

A few seconds later, I was typing away . . .

One of the great American novels of all time is . . .

Yes. You guessed it. I was writing a book report for Travis.

And when I finished this one, I planned to write a book report for Kelly.

You don't blame me—do you?

After the Kraken attack, I realized just how dangerous those two guys were. They didn't care what they did to me. And it took that vicious dog to prove it to me.

Having Travis and Kelly as enemies had become too dangerous.

Yes, cheating for them was risky. Writing their book reports could get me into the worst kind of trouble.

But at least I'd be *alive*!

I definitely decided it would be worth the risk if they would be my friends from now on.

Did I tell Lizzie about it? No, I didn't.

Lizzie was too sensible. And too afraid of doing anything bad.

She would tell me to go to my dad and tell him what Travis and Kelly did. And there was *no way* I would ever do that. Or, Lizzie would tell me to go see Mr. Plame and tell him about the deal the two boys wanted to make with me.

If I did anything like that, Travis and Kelly would become *even worse* enemies. Even more dangerous. My life would be over. I'd be as dead as that dummy lying on my bed.

I leaned into the glow of the laptop screen and typed away. I knew it wouldn't take me long to write it.

I also planned to write Kelly's report tonight. It wouldn't take me more than an hour.

I was concentrating so hard, I didn't hear someone enter my room and walk up behind me. "Huh?" I gasped when I felt a tap on my shoulder.

I spun around and blinked at my dad. "Hi."

He chuckled. "You were working so hard, you didn't even look up." He squinted at the screen. "Barton, what are you writing?"

I hesitated. "Uh . . . a book report," I said finally.

He turned his gaze on me. "Didn't you already write it?"

"I'm . . . uh . . . I'm doing another one," I stammered. "For extra credit."

That wasn't a lie. I was writing it for extra credit—extra credit from Travis and Kelly.

"You're a good student," Dad said. He started to leave, but then he turned back. "Barton, I've been meaning to ask you about those two boys. You know. The ones who were picking on you and giving you a tough time?"

I nodded. "No worries, Dad," I said. "I'm

taking care of them. They won't be picking on me anymore."

"Good," Dad said. "Glad to hear it. Glad you handled it." He turned and vanished downstairs.

"Oh, yes. I'm handling it," I said, returning to the book report for Travis. "I'm taking care of it."

Did it all work out the way I had hoped?

Not exactly.

15

"I'm very pleased with the job you people did on your final book reports," Mr. Plame said. "Many of you did your best work of the year. That's something to be proud of, everyone."

It was one week later, and he was passing back our reports with a grade on them.

Was I tense? Was I shaking in my seat?

Well, yes. Not because of *my* report. I knew I'd get an A. I can't help it. Writing is just easy for me.

I was jittery and nervous and jumpy and frightened and totally freaking out because of Travis and Kelly. What grades would they get? Did Mr. Plame figure out that something smelled here? That something was different about their book reports?

Had he guessed that serious cheating had taken place?

Was I about to face the firing squad? Suspension from school forever?

The teacher moved down the aisle of desks, handing back the reports, making short comments to each kid.

"Good job."

"You really surprised me with this one."

"I think you had some good ideas here. But you need to flesh them out. Explain your point of view better."

Then he stopped beside Travis.

My heart stopped. I couldn't breathe. I watched him hand the report to Travis. What was he going to say? *We need to talk? Meet me in the principal's office?*

I stared in horror as Mr. Plame gave Travis a tap on the shoulder. "Travis, this is by far your best work in my class," he said.

Travis took the paper from Mr. Plame. He blinked a few times.

"I especially liked your comments about how dramatic irony is used," Mr. Plame said.

"Yeah. I thought a lot about that," Travis said.

Liar.

Mr. Plame stopped at Kelly's desk next, and I continued to hold my breath.

"You did good work, too," he told him. "What made you decide to choose this book, Kelly?"

Kelly thought for a long moment. "I liked the cover," he said finally.

That made Mr. Plame laugh. A few kids laughed, too.

"Well, I liked what you had to say about the author's crisp writing style," Mr. Plame said. "Your comparisons were excellent, Kelly. I didn't realize you like to read so much."

"Yeah. I'm into reading," Kelly said.

Mr. Plame moved to the next desk, and I started to breathe again.

I'm getting away with it, I thought. *I cheated and I'm getting away with it.*

I felt a bump on my shoulder and turned. Lizzie leaned across the aisle and whispered to me: "What's up with that? Do you believe those two jerks wrote good book reports?"

I nodded. "Yes. I believe it."

The rest of the day seemed just fine. But when I started to walk home, Travis and Kelly were waiting for me in the teachers' parking lot.

"Hey, Sluggs," Travis called. "We want to talk to you."

I followed them to the fence at the back of the parking lot. They each had a bag of tortilla chips, and they crunched chips as they walked. I thought they might offer me some, but they didn't.

"Hey, thanks for writing those papers," Travis said. "First A-minus I ever got."

"And how come I only got a B?" Kelly demanded. He swallowed the last chip, crinkled the bag up, and tossed it at my chest. "Why didn't you get me an A, Sluggs?"

I took a step back. "I . . . did the best I could," I told him. "You never get B's, Kelly. I know you don't even get C's."

Kelly curled his fists at his sides. "You were supposed to get us A's."

"That wasn't the deal," I said. "Come on. I saved your lives. I saved your final grades. I can't believe you're giving me a hard time."

Travis gave Kelly a hard shove, sending him

back into the fence. "Shut up, Kelly. Sluggs is right. He did an awesome job."

Kelly tried to shove Travis back. But Travis dodged to the side, and Kelly missed.

I decided to change the subject. "Hey, guys, tell me about the Crokodile Tears concert. How are we getting to the civic center? Are your parents driving you there? Can you pick me up?"

They both stared at me.

"You're joking, right?" Travis said.

"No. Why?"

"The concert was last week," Travis said. "You missed it, Sluggs."

"You should have gone. It was totally *awesome*!" Kelly exclaimed.

"No, wait—" I said. "You said you had a ticket for me. You said—"

"No, we didn't," Kelly said.

"I don't remember anything about a ticket," Travis said.

"No. Come on," I said. "Seriously. Stop kidding around. You promised. You promised we'd go. You promised we'd be friends. We'd hang out at the concert."

"We said that? Are you sure?" Kelly said.

"That was a joke," Travis said. He grinned at me. "Don't you know when we're joking?"

"Why would we hang out with a slug?" Kelly said.

They both laughed.

I let out a long sigh. I suddenly felt weak. Dizzy.

It was all a trick. They tricked me into writing their papers. And they lied. They were lying about the whole deal.

I risked everything for them, and they were lying the whole time. It was all a joke . . . just a mean joke.

"I—I—I—" I was too angry to talk. I could feel the anger growing inside me, burning my chest, growing . . . growing . . . until I was about to burst apart. Explode like a big balloon popping.

"You TRICKED me!" I screamed. And then I lost it.

I went diving into Kelly. I tackled him hard, and he crashed to the ground. Then Travis tried to pull me off Kelly, and he tripped over my legs.

"HEY, STOP THAT!" a voice shouted. "WHAT ARE YOU DOING?"

Panting hard, I looked up. And saw Mr. Plame running full speed across the parking lot. His face was bright red and his eyes were wide with surprise.

He was out of breath by the time he stopped in front of me. "Barton? I . . . I don't believe what I just saw," he stammered.

"Barton attacked us," Travis said, picking himself up off the ground.

"He just went berserk," Kelly added.

"It . . . it was an accident," I said.

Totally lame. But I was too stunned to think clearly.

Mr. Plame turned to Kelly and Travis. They both were groaning and holding their stomachs and acting like they'd never recover.

"Are you okay?" the teacher asked them.

"No," they both said at the same time.

"I think he broke my ribs," Kelly groaned.

What a phony.

"Let's get you both to the nurse," Mr. Plame said. He turned back to me. "I saw the whole thing. I saw you lunge at Kelly. Why on earth did you do that, Barton?"

I lowered my head. "It's a long story," I muttered.

Mr. Plame wiped sweat off his forehead with the back of his hand. He narrowed his eyes at me. "You know we have a zero-tolerance violence policy at this school."

"Yeah. I know," I said.

He took my arm. "Okay. Come to the office and let's call your parents."

SLAPPY HERE, EVERYONE

Haha. Looks like our friend Barton got himself in some serious trouble. Doesn't he know Rule Number One?

Always tackle someone when your teacher ISN'T looking!

I learned that in kindergarten. I was a real star in kindergarten. That's because all the others in my class were *dummies*! Hahaha.

Well . . . you'd better turn the page. This story is about to get good. That's because the rest of it is about ME! Hahahaha.

17

"It's about time you got back at those two bullies!" Dad exclaimed at dinner that night.

I tried to tell him it was all a mistake. An accident.

Mrs. Garvey, the middle school principal, suspended me from school for a week. And Dad was the only one who was happy about it.

"You shouldn't encourage violence," Mom said, shaking her head.

"Those two punks won't be bothering Barton anytime soon," Dad replied.

I didn't think he was right. But I kept my head lowered to my spaghetti bowl.

"They're kids. They're not punks," Mom said.

"This spaghetti is cold," Dad complained. "How on earth do you make cold spaghetti?"

"*You* cooked dinner tonight!" Mom said. "Did you forget?"

She and Dad started shouting at each other

about which one of them made the spaghetti. I ate quickly and hurried upstairs to my room.

A whole week without school. Some kids might be happy about that. But not me. Being suspended from school was bad news. And I wasn't even being punished for writing those two book reports. I was suspended for fighting. I couldn't believe it.

I pictured Travis and Kelly in the parking lot that afternoon. I pictured them both on the ground.

"It's all their fault," I murmured to myself. "If they hadn't played such a mean trick . . ."

And now everyone was upset and disappointed in me. Mrs. Garvey was upset. Mr. Plame was so upset, he could barely speak. Mom was so upset, she pretended it was perfectly normal for me to be home all day.

And I wondered if Lizzie was unhappy with me, too. I tried texting her, but she didn't reply. Maybe she hadn't even heard about it.

Sighing, I slumped to the closet and pulled the dummy out of its case. I carried it to the edge of my bed and sat it down on my lap.

"Slappy," I said, "you may be my only friend."

The dummy grinned back at me with its painted smile.

I reached into the jacket pocket and pulled out the two sheets of paper. I folded up the first one and tucked it back into the pocket. Then I raised the page with the funny words to my face.

"What do these words mean?" I asked out loud.

I started to read them. But I heard footsteps on the stairs—and Lizzie burst into my room.

She was dressed in a short white skirt and a white top. She had obviously just come from a tennis lesson. Her dark hair fell wildly around her face.

"Barton—I heard," she said. "Are you okay?"

I shrugged. "Yeah. Fine."

Lizzie took a moment to catch her breath. "My mom heard about you from one of her friends."

"Good news travels fast," I said sarcastically.

"You're making jokes?" she cried. "You were suspended from school and you're making jokes?"

I shrugged. "What else can I do?"

She swept her hair back with both hands. "Did you really attack Travis and Kelly?"

"Well . . . we all ended up on the ground," I said. "I didn't really attack them."

Her mouth dropped open and stayed open. "I—I—I—"

"I know. You're shocked," I said.

"How long are you suspended?"

"A week," I said.

"Oh, wow. Oh, wow. How are your parents taking it?" she asked.

"One good, one bad," I said. "Dad thinks I'm a superhero. Mom thinks I'm a criminal."

She squinted at the dummy on my lap. “Hey, what are you doing with that thing?”

“Just goofing,” I said. “I have a lot of time to fill. Maybe if I work up a ventriloquist act, it will take my mind off what happened. And I think I can use him for my History project.”

“Use the dummy? How?”

“I'm doing the history of puppets,” I said. “I can do a thing about ventriloquist dummies, too.” I bounced Slappy in my lap. “What are you doing for your History project?”

Lizzie dragged my desk chair over to the bed and sat down across from me. “I'm going to show off some of my more unusual stuffed dogs,” she said. “And I'm going to talk about how dogs came to be pets for humans. It's interesting. Dogs came out of the wild and started being pets thousands of years ago.

“What's that paper in your hand?” Lizzie pointed.

I didn't realize I was still holding it. “Some weird words,” I said. “They came with the dummy.”

“Words?” Lizzie grabbed the paper from my hand.

“Hey, these *are* weird words.” She raised the page and read the words out loud: “KARRU MARRI ODONNA LOMA MOLONU KARRANO.”

And that's when things got crazy.

I heard a soft buzz and felt something like an electric current roll through the dummy. I sat him up straight.

His eyes blinked.

I didn't do it. I wasn't controlling his eyes.

Lizzie handed the sheet of paper to me, and I stuffed it back in Slappy's jacket pocket. "Is that supposed to be some kind of magic spell?"

"I don't know," I said.

And then the dummy's wooden lips clicked up and down. "This is where the magic happens!" he rasped.

Lizzie gasped. "I didn't know you could throw your voice, Barton."

"I—I can't!" I stammered. "Slappy said that. I didn't."

"Shut up," Lizzie snapped. "Don't try to freak me out."

We both stared at the grinning dummy.

"He sure is ugly," Lizzie said.

"You're not so cute yourself!" Slappy cried in a high, shrill voice.

Lizzie frowned at me. "Is that supposed to be funny?"

"I—I didn't say it," I stammered. I could feel the blood pulsing at my temples. Something weird was happening here.

I really wasn't saying those things. I knew Lizzie wouldn't believe me. But the dummy was talking on his own.

"Are you sure you should wear white?" Slappy shouted at Lizzie. "You look like a used tissue!"

"Stop it, Barton," Lizzie snapped. "You're not funny. You have to practice and think up better jokes."

"Are those your lips?" Slappy asked Lizzie. "Or are you eating worms? Hahahaha!"

Lizzie jumped up and sent the desk chair sliding back across the room. "I'm outta here," she said.

"No, wait—" I stood up, holding Slappy in one hand. "You've got to believe me. I—"

"We've been friends since fourth grade," Lizzie said. "I thought I knew you. But . . . you're totally weird, Barton. First, you attack two kids and get kicked out of school. Then you start pretending a dummy can talk and say really gross things to me. And—and—oh, good-bye."

She turned and strode out of the room.

I stood without moving and listened to her hurry down the stairs and out the front door.

I turned the dummy toward me and raised it so we were eye to eye.

"She's cute," Slappy rasped. "What species is she?"

"You can really talk!" I cried. "You're alive!"

I raised him high above my head. "You're alive! Alive!"

"Put me down!" the dummy screamed. "Do you hear me? Put me down!"

I lowered him till we were face-to-face again. My brain was spinning. I could barely breathe.

I knew I should be *terrified* of this creature. But I wasn't.

I suddenly had plans for him. I didn't even have to think about it for a second. The idea flashed into my brain, and I knew the dummy could change my life.

Holding him in front of me, I felt as if I had won a lottery. I was the new champion of the world! I was unbeatable! Immortal!

Slappy was about to become my new secret weapon. My new way to finally get my revenge against Travis and Kelly.

The dummy blinked its eyes a few times. "What's wrong with you?" he snapped. "You're supposed to be scared of me."

"Scared?" I replied. "Why?"

"Because I'm *alive*," he said. "Because I can do really bad things. Because I can do really bad things to *you*!"

I snickered. "I can do bad things to you, too, Slappy. I can put you back in your case."

"No, you can't," he rasped in his scratchy, shrill voice. "Try it."

"Okay." I swung him over my shoulder and walked to the closet. I bent and pulled the case from the closet floor. Then I started to pull up the lid.

"Owwwwww!"

I screamed as a powerful electric current buzzed over both my hands. I could see the electricity zapping over my skin. Pain shot up and down my arms.

"Okay! Okay!" I shouted. "I get it. You can do bad things."

Slappy rolled his eyes, and the current stopped crackling over me. I shook both hands in the air. They still buzzed and throbbed.

"*Now* are you scared of me?" the dummy asked.

"Okay, okay," I mumbled. "So you've got powers. That's even better."

The dummy's eyes spun in his head. "Better? Why is that better?"

"Because you're going to help me," I said. "We're going to be best buddies."

"No, we're not," he insisted. "Someone must have scrambled your brain—if you have one. We're not going to be friends. You're going to be my servant. Servant for life!"

I laughed. "Sounds great."

The dummy blinked at me. "Are you kidding me? You should be shaking right now."

"I *am* shaking," I said. "Shaking with laughter. You're funny."

"Maybe you need another shock treatment from me," Slappy said.

I sat him on the bed and held him up by the shoulders. I brought my face close to his. "Don't you understand?" I said. "Thanks to you, I own the only living dummy on earth! You're going to make me famous. And there are a few other things you are going to do for me. There are two guys I want you to meet."

The dummy shook his head. "You need a checkup from the neck up, kid. *Everyone* is scared of me. Do you hear? *Everyone!*"

"You and I are going to be good friends," I said. "Forget that scare stuff. It won't work on me. Save it for these two guys in my class. You can get as scary as you like with them."

I patted him on the top of his wooden head. "I am your friend," I said, "and friends don't scare friends."

Boy, was I wrong.

19

All week, I thought about the ways I could use Slappy to scare Travis and Kelly. Slappy chuckled at every evil idea I had.

I saw that he could be dangerous. But I thought as long as I stayed his friend, I'd be okay.

On Friday night, I invited Lizzy to come work on our science notebooks. But that was a lie. I wanted to tell her all about Slappy and the plans I had for my new friend.

I greeted her at the front door. Her mouth dropped open in shock. "Barton? What happened to your hair?" she asked. "It looks like you stuck your head in a blender!"

"No big deal," I said. "Travis and Kelly caught me after school. They said they had to give me a Welcome Back to School present. Then they held me down and gave me a haircut."

Lizzie gasped. "Huh? Aren't you upset? What did your parents say?"

"They didn't notice," I said.

"But—but—" Lizzie sputtered. "You can't let those boys get away with that."

"Don't worry about it," I said, leading the way upstairs to my room. "I've got a plan for them."

"A plan? What are you going to do? Go after them again?"

"You'll see," I said. I closed the door behind us. I motioned for Lizzie to take a seat on my desk chair.

"Why are you grinning like that, Barton?" she demanded. "Have you looked in a mirror? Have you seen what they did to you?"

"No worries, Lizzie. They're history. You'll see."

"Are you going to tell me your plan?"

I shook my head. "No. I'm going to show you. I'll give you a hint. Slappy is going to help out."

She rolled her eyes. "Oh, sure. Great plan, Barton. An old ventriloquist dummy will help you get revenge against Travis and Kelly. Do you have a thermometer up here? I think you're running a fever."

I motioned for her to come over to the closet. "You'll see," I said.

"I know what's in your closet," Lizzie said. "Puppets. Is that what you're going to do? Put on a puppet show for Travis and Kelly? Wow. That'll teach them a lesson."

"I'm not going to do a puppet show," I said. "I'm going to put on a *Slappy* show."

She stepped up beside me. I grabbed the closet door handle. "You're not going to believe this," I said.

I pulled open the closet door—and gasped.

Slappy was gone.

20

I stepped into the closet. I had a bunch of marionettes hanging on hooks against the closet wall. I pushed them aside and peered to the back. No sign of him.

"That's weird," I said, turning to Lizzie. "I left him here this morning."

"BOOOO!" a shrill voice shouted.

I jumped. Lizzie and I stumbled out of the closet and spun toward the voice. "Greetings!" Slappy called.

Lizzie uttered a sharp cry. "Barton? How are you doing this? How do you make him walk?"

"I . . . I'm not doing it," I stammered.

I'd been with him the whole week I was home. But I had no idea he could walk. *Awesome!* I thought. *This is even better than I had imagined!*

The dummy walked awkwardly. His legs were soft and rubbery as his hard shoes clomped across my bedroom floor.

"Why are you trying to scare me?" Lizzie inched away from the dummy.

"Yes, why are you trying to scare her?" Slappy rasped. He tossed back his head and laughed.

The dummy stopped in the middle of the room. "Where did you two meet? At a Nerd Circus? Hahaha."

Lizzie grabbed my arm. Her hand was ice-cold. "Are you . . . making him talk?"

"Hey, who's working *your* head?" Slappy asked her. He turned to me. "Look out, Barton. Someone dropped a pile of fish guts on your head. Oh, wait—is that your *hair*? Hahaha."

I laughed, too. "Good one, Slappy," I said.

"Barton, if you got down on all fours, you could enter yourself in an Ugly Dog contest!" he shouted. "You'd WIN!"

I laughed again. "You're funny, Slappy," I said.

Lizzie poked me hard in the side. "I don't think he's funny. I think he's terrifying."

Slappy nodded. "She's got the right idea, Barton. I *am* terrifying!"

"I *want* you to be terrifying," I said. "We talked about it all week, remember? You're my new friend, Slappy. And I *need* you to be terrifying."

"He . . . he's not your friend," Lizzie stammered. "He's a dummy!"

"Don't call me DUMMY, dummy!" Slappy screamed in a sudden rage. He shot his hands above his head and uttered a long, angry howl.

"I'm out of here!" Lizzie cried. She bolted toward the door. But Slappy moved quickly to block her path.

She stumbled into him, and the two of them toppled to the floor.

"Oh no! Oh no!" Lizzie cried as she scrambled to her feet.

"Don't go," Slappy said, sitting up. "The party is just getting started."

"Party?" Lizzie shook her head.

"Well, it's a party for *me*," Slappy said. "Let's play a great party game. It's called *Slappy's Servants for Life*! The servants are you two. And the game will last for the rest of your lives! Hahaha!"

"No way!" Lizzie cried. She jumped over Slappy and burst out of the room. Her shoes thudded loudly down the stairs. The front door slammed behind her.

I took a few steps toward the grinning dummy. "Slappy, you scared her to death," I said.

Slappy shook his head. "It's weird. Sometimes I have that effect on people! Hahaha!"

"Well, Lizzie isn't the one you're supposed to scare," I said. "She's my friend. You're supposed to scare Travis and Kelly."

The dummy's eyes appeared to glow. "I'll scare whoever I want *whenever* I want!" he screamed.

The dummy walked slowly toward me. "Think you're so brave, *friend*? Haha. *Everyone* is scared of Slappy. And now it's *your* turn."

21

"Be scared, Barton," Slappy said, lowering his voice to a growl. "Be very scared."

He raised his hands and I froze. I struggled to move my arms, my legs. But he had cast a spell on them or something. I couldn't move.

He raised his hands higher—and my hands shot up, too.

He made his hands wiggle in the air. And *my* hands wiggled in the air.

He bent his legs. My legs bent, too.

He was completely controlling me!

"Be scared! Be very scared!" he repeated.

Then he waved his hands in a circle. And I began to dance. A wild tap dance. My shoes clattered over the floor as I danced.

Slappy tossed back his head and laughed. "You're MY puppet now, Barty, old boy!"

He swung his hands down low. And I collapsed to the floor in a heap.

"You're MY puppet now. How does it feel?"

I tried to stand up. But he kept me down on the floor.

"Feels awesome!" I said. "What an awesome trick. I love it!"

The dummy's mouth fell open. He appeared to be speechless.

"Barton, are you afraid to admit that you are *terrified*?" Slappy said finally.

I shook my head. "I'm not terrified," I said. "I think you're funny. We're going to have a great time. I can't wait for Travis and Kelly to meet you. This is so much better than I had expected. Slappy, my friend, I can't wait."

"Stop calling me *friend*!" Slappy screamed. "You're going to be scared of me. *Everyone* is scared of Slappy! And it's your turn. It's your turn, Barton!"

I heard a soft squeak. I turned in time to see the closet door swing open.

I gasped as the first marionette came walking stiffly out of the closet. It was my soldier puppet in a khaki uniform. The puppet walked slowly as if sleepwalking. Its hands were stuck straight in front of it . . . like a zombie!

Two more of my puppets—a princess and a clown—came marching out of the closet. Their black eyes stared straight ahead of them. Their arms were outstretched as they moved slowly toward me in a line.

And then two more marionettes. *All* my marionettes were out, alive! Marching stiffly, silently. Wooden puppets brought to life by Slappy.

Again, I struggled to stand up. But a powerful force kept me down on the floor.

The puppets marched in a line and formed a circle around me. Around and around, they moved faster as they circled me.

And then their wooden hands began to move, swinging at me.

Slap slap slap.

They slapped my face hard as they marched around me, their bodies stiff, their wooden shoes thumping the floor.

Slap slap.

I raised a hand to protect my face. But Slappy forced my hand back down to my side. And the puppets continued to slap me. Harder. Faster.

"Ow!" I cried out in pain. Helpless, I struggled to move away from them.

Slap slap slap slap.

My face stung with pain. I opened my mouth in a horrified scream.

I heard the dummy's high-pitched laugh.

"I *knew* I could scare you, Barton! But that's nothing. That's just a warm-up! Watch THIS!"

Slappy waved a hand and the puppets stopped marching.

One final slap—and then they all lowered their hands.

I tried one more time to stand up. But Slappy was using his power to hold me there.

"Let me up!" I shouted. "Let me up, Slappy!"

Before I could say any more, the puppets all leaped at once.

Their soft legs bent—and they *jumped* high. Jumped onto me.

"Hey—!" I fell onto my back, and they swarmed over me.

"It's WAR!" Slappy screamed at the top of his voice. "Let the BATTLE begin! Hahahaha!"

I was too stunned to cry out as a wooden puppet hand tugged hard at my nose. Another marionette gripped my hair and pulled so hard, tears streamed down my cheeks.

Puppets poked and tugged and slapped at me.

It felt as if they were trying to pull the top of my head off.

A marionette tried to move my eyelids up and down. Another one forced my mouth to open and close—*like a puppet!* I struggled to squirm free. But I was being kicked and slapped, and I couldn't move.

And all the while, I could hear Slappy's shrill laugh ringing off the walls.

Then, to my surprise, the marionettes pulled back and began to circle me. Marching in a fast rhythm, they wrapped their strings around me, trapping me in a tight cocoon. The strings tightened around my waist . . . my chest . . . my head.

"Please—" I choked out. "Slappy, please—"

Their strings loosened and fell away. They all froze. As if given a command.

Silently, the marionettes dropped to the floor and lay in a motionless heap.

Once again, I heard the dummy's shrill laughter, crazy, evil laughter.

I sucked in breath after breath. Slowly, the pain faded from my chest, my head stopped throbbing, and my eyes began to focus again.

I lifted myself onto one elbow. My whole body was trembling. I took more deep breaths.

The dummy stood over me, peering down, that painted grin wide across his face. "Well, Barton?" he rasped. "Still want to be *friends*? Or are you scared of me now?"

"I—I—" I tried to speak, but my throat ached and I started to choke.

Slappy laughed. "Yes, you get it now. You see my power, and you're smart enough to be scared."

Rubbing my aching throat, I struggled to my feet. Now I was peering down at Slappy.

Yes, he's terrifying, I thought. *But I need him. I can't let him see how afraid I am.*

So I forced myself to sound calm. "You're funny," I said. "Did you really think that was scary? A bunch of puppets marching around? That makes me laugh."

"Liar!" he snapped. "I know you're scared. All kids are scared of me. When they find out they will be my servant for life, they are *terrified*! They'll do anything they can to get rid of me!"

I crossed my arms over my chest. "Not scared," I said. "I'm your friend, Slappy, and you're my friend."

He uttered an angry squawk.

I shoved my hands into my pockets so he wouldn't see them trembling. I had a plan, and I needed him. And *no way* would I admit to him that he was the least bit frightening.

"Don't you see I'm *evil*, Barty? Don't you see I'm all about one thing—evil!"

"Then I'm evil, too," I said. "We're going to be evil together, Slappy."

I grabbed him around the waist and tossed him onto the bed.

Startled, he sat up instantly with an angry growl.

"I'm not like the other kids," I said. "I'm your friend. Your evil friend! Haha! We're going to do great things together!"

23

Late that night, I was in bed, whispering on the phone to Lizzie.

"I'm sorry you got scared," I said. "He's pretty scary."

"A dummy coming to life?" Lizzie replied. "That's like a horror movie, Barton."

"I know," I said. "But I need him. I have a plan."

"Barton, listen to me," she whispered. "Forget your plan. You have an evil thing in your house. You have to get rid of it."

I heard footsteps out in the hall. Either Mom or Dad was going to bed. I held the phone tightly in my hand and waited for them to pass my room.

I'm not allowed to use my phone after nine at night. If Mom or Dad heard me talking to Lizzie now, my jeans pocket would be empty for a long time. No phone.

"Of course I'm going to get rid of him," I whispered to Lizzie when it was silent out in the hall again. "But if he thinks we're friends, I can use him."

"For what?"

"To change my life," I said.

"What are you talking about? Travis and Kelly?"

"Yes," I said. "I'm going to use him to terrify those two jerks. If Slappy thinks he and I are best friends, he'll help me make sure Travis and Kelly never try anything against me again."

"So you're going to scare them," Lizzie whispered.

"I don't want to scare them," I said. "I want to *terrify* them. I'm giving my report about the history of puppets in class on Tuesday. I'm going to bring some puppets to school. And I'm going to bring Slappy."

"I get it," Lizzie whispered. "Travis and Kelly won't be able to resist. They'll start messing with the dummy—"

"And Slappy will go to work on them," I said. I couldn't help it. I started to giggle. "This is going to be so cool!"

Silence on the other end. I could hear Lizzie breathing. "But then what, Barton?" she whispered.

"Then what? I guess I'll have to get rid of Slappy."

"But how?" Lizzie demanded. "He's alive. He's dangerous. You can't just put him back in his case and leave him somewhere."

"I know," I said. "I already tried to put him in his case. It didn't work out so well."

"Maybe you could take his head off," Lizzie said. "That might stop him."

"That might work," I said. I yawned. My head suddenly felt like it weighed a hundred pounds. I couldn't think straight about getting rid of the dummy. "I'm getting sleepy," I said. "See you tomorrow."

I clicked the phone off and set it down on my bed table. Then I turned onto my side and pulled the covers up to my chin.

I shut my eyes tight and tried to force Slappy from my mind. But his grinning face kept bobbing like a balloon before my eyes. I tried counting sheep. But the sheep all had Slappy's face. I tried counting down from one thousand.

Finally, I started to drift to sleep.

A squeak from across the room startled me. I sat straight up. And heard my closet door swing open. And then the soft pad of shoes across the carpet.

I blinked myself alert. "Slappy—what are you doing?" I choked out. "What do you want? Where are you going?"

He moved close to the bed. His green eyes appeared to glow in the dark. "Just wanted to check on you," he said.

"Huh?"

"You're my friend, Barton. I just wanted to make sure you were comfortable. Make sure you were sleeping okay."

"Uh . . . yeah. I'm fine," I said. "Thanks for checking on me. Good night, Slappy."

"Good night," he replied. He turned and shuffled back to the closet.

I lowered my head to the pillow. *It's working*, I thought. *He really thinks we're friends.*

This is going to be so much fun!

24

"People have been making puppets for longer than you think," I said. "Some books say that puppets have been around for four thousand years."

I moved the controller in my hand and made my soldier marionette walk toward Mr. Plame's desk. The class watched in silence.

In the back row, I saw that Travis and Kelly had grins on their faces. I knew they were just waiting to make fun of me. But I continued giving my report.

"I read that the Egyptians of four thousand years ago had marionettes carved of wood—just like the one I have here. They worked the strings to make the puppets look as if they were kneading bread."

"Did you bring any bread?" Travis shouted.

Some kids laughed. Mr. Plame raised a finger to his lips. "Don't interrupt, Travis."

"Puppets made of clay and ivory were found in

Egyptian tombs," I continued. "Some historians believe that theaters had puppet shows before there were even actors."

I made my soldier puppet take a bow. Then I draped it over the wooden chair I had carried to the front of the room. "I've been interested in puppets since I was a little kid," I said.

I held up the other puppet I had brought to show everyone. "This is a princess marionette," I said. "My dad got it for me. As you can see, the head isn't carved of wood. It's made of straw."

"Like your brain!" Kelly shouted.

Some kids laughed.

"Sluggs, where are *your* strings?" Travis called out.

Mr. Plame jumped to his feet. He pointed to Travis and Kelly. "Let's be polite, boys. Barton is giving a very interesting report."

He turned to Slappy. I had him sitting up on the floor with his back to the wall. "Tell us about this doll, Barton."

I picked Slappy up and cradled him between my arms. "This is a ventriloquist dummy," I said.

"Which one is the dummy?" Travis called. Big laughter.

Mr. Plame's cheeks reddened. "I'm warning you, Travis," he said.

"The word *ventriloquism* actually means *speaking from the stomach* in Latin," I said. "In ancient times, some people believed that dead people lived in your stomach. And a ventriloquist could bring their voices to life."

"That's very interesting," Mr. Plame said. "When did the dummies begin to be used for entertainment?"

"In the 1700s," I said. "People began doing ventriloquism at parties. At first, they didn't have puppets or dolls. They used their hands for puppets and talked to them. But then some people had the idea of using dolls."

"Barton, can you throw your voice?" Mr. Plame asked.

I shook my head. "Not really. I just got this dummy, and I haven't had time to practice."

Besides, he talks on his own, I thought. *He doesn't need me to put words in his mouth.*

"Well, thank you for an excellent report," Mr. Plame said. "I'm very impressed with the research you did, Barton."

"Thank you," I said.

I started to put Slappy down, but Mr. Plame reached for him. "Can I see him?"

I had no choice. I handed the dummy to the teacher. He held Slappy like a baby and stared down at his face. "He has such an evil grin," he said. "I wonder why the puppet-maker decided to carve such an ugly face."

I held my breath.

I saw Slappy blink his eyes. *Is he going to say something?*

That morning, I made Slappy promise not to talk. Not to move. To stay limp and lifeless like a normal wooden dummy.

He promised.

But Mr. Plame had just insulted him. And I saw Slappy blink. And my heart leaped into my mouth.

I gasped as the dummy's mouth dropped open.

Please don't say anything. Please don't move. Please, Slappy, don't do anything to Mr. Plame.

25

Slappy's mouth slid wide open—and then it clamped shut on Mr. Plame's pointer finger.

The teacher uttered a sharp cry. He grabbed the dummy's head and tried to pry his finger free. But Slappy's wooden lips remained shut tightly over it.

"Owwwww. This really hurts!" he cried.

He tried to twist his finger free. Then he gave a hard pull—and I heard a loud *craaack*.

"I . . . I think my finger's broken," Mr. Plame said. His face was flaming red now and twisted in pain.

He turned to me. "Barton—do something." He tried to shove the dummy at me. But Slappy's wooden lips were clamped tightly over the finger.

Kids were shouting and crying out in surprise.

I wrapped my hands around Slappy's head. "I'm sorry, Mr. Plame," I said. "It's an old dummy. I think the controls may be broken."

I shoved my hand into Slappy's back and

fumbled around until I found the mouth control. "I think the mouth spring is busted," I said.

I knew it wasn't the mouth spring. I knew it was Slappy being vicious. But I had to pretend he was like a normal dummy.

I tugged the string inside his back . . . tugged it . . . tugged it—and Slappy's mouth finally sprang open.

Mr. Plame sighed loudly and shook his finger in the air. It was red and swollen like a sausage. He jumped to his feet. "I'm going to run down the hall and see the nurse. I'm sure my finger is broken."

"I . . . I'm sorry," I stammered. I held Slappy by the neck, down at my side. "I hope this won't hurt my grade."

Mr. Plame didn't answer. He strode to the door and hurried out of the classroom.

Everyone started talking at once. I saw Travis and Kelly laughing their heads off and bumping knuckles.

The bell rang. Time to go home. I packed the two marionettes in the case I'd brought for them. And then I slung Slappy over my shoulder.

"You promised," I whispered to him. "You promised you wouldn't move."

The dummy blinked his eyes, but he didn't reply.

"Good report, Barton," Lizzy said. She swung her backpack over her shoulders. "Too bad about Mr. Plame's finger."

"Yeah. Too bad," I muttered.

The classroom had emptied out. "Are you walking home?" she asked.

"Uh . . . no," I said. "I have some things I have to do first."

She squinted at me. "Really?"

I nodded. "Yeah. Catch you later."

Lizzie shrugged and turned away. I watched her make her way out of the room.

I knew what was going to happen next. And I wanted to enjoy it all by myself.

I knew that Kelly had a dentist appointment. But I also knew that Travis would be waiting for me. Travis couldn't resist. I was sure of it. Travis was waiting to give me a hard time. To make fun of me and my puppets.

I knew he would be there.

And I was right.

He was waiting in the vacant lot on the next block. He leaned against a fat tree trunk with his legs crossed at his ankles. Like real casual. And his grin grew wider as I walked toward him.

I knew it. I knew it.

My heart started to pound because I knew I was about to wipe that grin off his face.

I knew it was time for my new best friend Slappy to go to work.

"Hey, Dummy Boy!" Travis called. He stepped away from the tree and came striding toward me. "Dummy Boy! How uncool can you be?"

"Travis, give me a break," I murmured.

He sneered at me. "Think you're so awesome because you have these stupid puppets?" He laughed. "You're twelve years old, and you're still playing with dolls!"

"Please," I murmured. "Just let me go home."

I tried to step around him. But he moved fast and blocked my path. Then he raised both hands—and shoved me back as hard as he could.

"Hey—!" I shouted as I struggled to keep my balance.

The puppet case hit the ground. The latch snapped open, and the puppets tumbled onto the grass. Slappy fell face-forward and landed on his stomach. His head bounced once. I saw his eyes blink.

Travis laughed some more. "You're such a klutz. I hardly touched you."

I didn't say anything. This was the moment I'd been waiting for.

"Go get him," I whispered to Slappy.

The dummy snapped to a sitting position, then jumped quickly to his feet. His jaw clicked up and down a few times, as if he was testing it.

Then he turned to Travis. "Did you know that *Travis* rhymes with *idiot*?" Slappy rasped.

Travis lowered his hands to his waist and studied the dummy. "How'd you do that, Sluggs?" he asked. "How did you make him stand up?"

"How do *you* stand up?" Slappy shouted. "Did your mother tie your shoes for you this morning?"

Travis squinted at me. "How did you do that? Some kind of remote control?"

"You're right about that, Travis!" Slappy exclaimed. "I have *control*! Watch what I can do!"

Slappy swung both hands high above his head.

I uttered a startled cry as Travis floated up from the ground.

His eyes went wide, and his mouth dropped open. He kicked his feet as he rose up in the air. "Hey—put me down! Put me DOWN!" he screamed.

Slappy swung his hands again, and Travis floated even higher.

I crossed my arms in front of me and watched. Travis was in a total panic now, so frightened he couldn't even scream. I couldn't keep a big smile from spreading across my face.

"He's like a big bird!" Slappy cried. "A dodo bird! Hahaha!"

Travis kicked and squirmed and waved his arms. He floated above our heads now. I had to bend my neck to see him.

"P-please—!" he choked out. "Please! Put me down!"

His face had darkened to purple. Big tears rolled down his cheeks.

I stepped up to Slappy. "Think it's time to let him down?"

"No way!" the dummy cried. "I'm just getting started. I saved my best stuff for now!"

"But, Slappy—" I protested.

He clasped both of his wooden hands together above his head. Then he moved them quickly in a wide circle.

"Nooooo!"

High above us, Travis screamed as he began to spin.

He twirled like a top, slowly at first, then picking up speed. Around and around he went, his hands shooting out at his sides as he spun.

"Please—!" he wailed. "I . . . I'm getting dizzy! I'm going to be *sick*!"

Slappy laughed. "Your *face* is making *me* sick!" he shouted up to Travis.

The dummy swung his hands again, and Travis stopped in midair. Then he began to spin in the other direction.

"Barton—please!" Travis cried. "Let me down! I'm begging you!"

Slappy made him spin even faster. So fast his cell phone flew out of his pocket and sailed into the trees.

I cupped my hands around my mouth and shouted up to him as loud as I could. "Do you really want to come down?"

"Yes!" he screamed. "Yes! Please!"

"Then swear you won't ever mess with me again!" I yelled.

"I swear! I swear!" he cried. "Never! I promise!"

He was spinning so hard, both of his shoes came flying off. They thudded to the ground next to me.

I turned to Slappy. "Okay. Let him down."

Slappy didn't move. He kept his hands twirling above his head.

"Let him down, Slappy," I repeated. "Good work. You've done it. He won't mess with me again."

Slappy ignored me and kept him spinning.

I grabbed the shoulder of the dummy's jacket. "Let Travis down," I insisted. "Do you hear me? Let him down now."

"You're joking," Slappy said, turning his evil grin on me. "He's been mean to you, my friend. I don't like people who hurt my friend."

"But, Slappy—"

Slappy tossed back his head and laughed. "Barty, my friend, I saved the best for last. Watch THIS!"

27

"Slappy, please—" I begged. But I couldn't stop him.

He called out some strange words and shot his arms down to his sides.

"Whoooooaaaah!" High above our heads, Travis screamed as he went sailing toward the tall tree in the middle of the lot. He spun his arms crazily, trying to stop himself.

But he was totally in Slappy's control.

I gasped as Travis landed hard on his knees on the top limb of the tree. The branch bent and made a cracking sound.

Was it about to break off?

No. It held.

With another scream, Travis tumbled off the high tree limb. He stopped his fall by grabbing it with both hands. Now he was hanging on to the limb, his face twisted in horror.

Leaves came flying off. Small branches fell to the ground.

"He—he's going to fall!" I stammered. "Slappy—he'll get hurt!"

Slappy snickered. "That will teach him to mess with my friend!"

"No!" I cried. "Get him down! You can't do that! You can't leave him hanging up there!"

Slappy turned his grin on me. "Let's go home, friend." He turned and started to walk away.

"No. Come back—!" I shouted.

"What an awesome day!" Slappy exclaimed. "Come on. Let's go home, friend."

My heart was pounding. This wasn't at all what I wanted. I wanted to scare Travis. I didn't want to *kill* him!

I spun back to the tree and gazed up at the top. Travis had pulled himself back up onto the heavy limb. He sat there, hunched, straddling the branch and clinging to it with both hands.

"I can't get down from here!" Travis shouted. "Barton, help me! Don't leave me up here!"

I pulled out my phone. "I . . . I'm calling 911!" I shouted up at Travis. "I'll call the fire department!"

I punched in the emergency number and told them where to find Travis. Then I gathered up my marionettes and hurried to catch up with Slappy. "That wasn't right. You went too far!" I told him.

Slappy laughed. "Too far isn't always far enough!" he said.

What did THAT mean?

"You can't walk," I said. "People will see you." I picked him up by the waist and slung him over my shoulder.

I crossed the street and headed for home. The afternoon sun was lowering behind the trees. A cool breeze felt good on my face, which was burning hot.

My heart was still fluttering in my chest. I kept picturing Travis up at the top of that tree. "How's he going to get down?" I asked Slappy.

The dummy's head bounced against my back as we walked. "That's his problem," he answered. "He shouldn't have been mean to my friend Barty."

"I hope the fire department has a ladder that's tall enough to rescue him," I said.

"Forget about him," Slappy replied. "He's history. You think *that* was bad? Wait till you see what I have planned for your friend Kelly!"

28

The house was empty. Mom and Dad were still at work.

I carried Slappy and the marionettes up to my room and hung the marionettes in my closet. I stared at Slappy. What did he have planned for Kelly? Did I make a huge mistake telling Slappy about Travis and Kelly?

I propped him up on my windowsill. "You'll be comfortable here," I said. "We'll talk later about Kelly. Don't do anything till we talk. Promise?"

He raised his right hand. "Promise. Anything for a friend."

I sat down at my desk and pulled my math textbook from my backpack. I knew I wouldn't be able to concentrate on my homework. But I had to try.

I kept picturing Travis spinning high in the air. And I kept seeing him sail helplessly onto the high tree branch, and hang there . . . hang there for dear life.

"Haha. Kelly is next," Slappy interrupted my thoughts. "And who comes after Kelly? You have to give me a list, Barty."

"No one comes next!" I said. "Kelly, then that's it. We're done."

"No way. We won't be done. I'll *never* stop protecting you. I've never had a real friend before. Everyone has always been scared of me."

He sighed. "You're the first one who understands me, Barty. You're my first friend. And I'm going to protect you from now on."

I stared back at him. I didn't really know what to say. "Thanks," I murmured.

Of course, I couldn't tell him what I was really thinking. After we taught Kelly a lesson, Slappy was going bye-bye.

He was dangerous. He was evil. And he had frightening powers.

He said he was my friend now. But I knew there was no way I could trust him.

What if he turned against me? What if something I did made him angry, and he decided to go after me?

The thought sent a shiver to the back of my neck.

He slumped back against the window. He shut his eyes, and his head dropped forward. Instantly asleep? Very strange.

I opened my math textbook and thumbed through to the assignment. But the front doorbell interrupted me.

It must be Lizzie, I thought. *Maybe she wants to do the math together.*

I hurried down the stairs and pulled open the front door.

Not Lizzie.

I uttered a gasp of surprise—and stared out at Travis, his dad, and a blue-uniformed police officer. They weren't smiling. In fact, they had really grim expressions on their faces as they stared back at me.

Travis had bandages on his hands and a dark bruise on his forehead.

"Are you Barton Suggs?" the police officer asked. He had a hard, scratchy voice, almost whispery.

"Uh . . . yes," I answered.

"Well, Barton," he said, "may we come in? We need to have a serious talk with you."

29

I led them into the living room. My legs felt a little rubbery, and I could feel the blood pulsing at my temples.

Of course, I knew why they were there.

Travis kept giving me cold stares. Like he was trying to destroy me with his magic eye rays. Mr. Fox kept a hand on Travis's shoulder. They both sat down side by side on the couch.

"I'm Officer Marcus," the policeman said. He pulled off his cap as he dropped into the leather armchair that faced the couch. He had short blond hair and crinkled-up blue eyes and freckles around his nose. He looked like a teenager. But he had to be older.

I sat on the hard, dark wooden chair that no one ever sits on. I clasped my hands tightly in my lap to stop them from shaking.

"Are your parents home?" the officer asked, looking around.

"Not yet," I said. I tried to keep my voice low and steady.

"Well, this won't take long," Officer Marcus said. "We need—"

"We need to know the story," Mr. Fox interrupted. "The truth." He squeezed Travis's shoulder.

Travis just kept staring darts at me.

"The truth?" I repeated. My brain whirred. *No way* they'd believe the truth.

"The fire department had a very hard time getting Travis down from that tree," Officer Marcus said. "I know you know what tree I'm talking about, Barton. I know you were there. We traced your 911 call."

I nodded. I didn't know what to say.

"Travis told me a crazy story," Mr. Fox said. "He claims you used some kind of a puppet to make him fly up to the top of that tree."

"Puppet?" I said. I avoided Travis's stare.

"He claims your puppet has magic powers," Mr. Fox continued. "I know it's a ridiculous story. But I reported it to the police anyway."

He leaned toward me in the chair. "Travis got caught up at the top of that tree *somehow*. And he says you're responsible."

My brain was doing flip-flops in my head. I knew I had to lie my way out of this. "I don't get it," I said. "Do you really think I have magic powers?"

Travis jumped to his feet. "You know you did it!" he shouted at me, shaking a fist at me. "You know it was that dummy. That dummy is alive. And he forced me into the air, and made me spin, and sent me flying onto the tree limb."

Officer Marcus motioned with one hand. "Sit down, Travis," he said softly. "Let's stay calm and not shout. Let's just get to the bottom of this."

Travis scowled at me. He dropped back onto the couch. His hands were still balled into fists.

"Travis, can you tell us the truth?" his dad asked. "The magical dummy story is just too impossible."

"But it's *true*!" Travis insisted.

Officer Marcus turned to Mr. Fox. "Sir, has your son been watching a lot of horror movies lately?"

"I'm not making it up! It's not a movie!" Travis screamed.

"Did you climb the tree?" his dad asked. "And you couldn't get down. So you're making up this story because you're embarrassed?"

"Dad, listen to me," Travis begged. "I'm not making it up. The dummy waved his hands in the air, and I went flying. You've *got* to believe me."

Mr. Fox turned to the officer. "I'm sorry to waste your time like this, but—"

"I have an idea," Officer Marcus said. "Barton, can we see the dummy? Do you have it?"

"It's upstairs in my room," I said. "I'm sorry Travis is so upset."

"No, you're not!" he screamed. "You're *not* sorry!"

Officer Marcus motioned for Travis to calm down. "Could you bring the dummy down?" he asked me. "I think if we show it to Travis, maybe he'll start to remember things differently."

"No problem," I said. I jumped up from the chair and made my way to the stairs.

In my room, I lifted Slappy off the windowsill. "Not a word out of you," I told him. "Do you hear me? Don't blink. Don't talk. Don't do anything. I'm serious."

He blinked his eyes. "Anything for a friend, Barty, my man."

I lifted him to my shoulder. "This wouldn't have happened if you hadn't gone too far."

"I'll always go too far for *you*," he said.

"Shut up, Slappy. I mean it," I whispered.

I carried him down to the living room. He hung limply over my shoulder, his arms and legs dangling in the air.

"This is my ventriloquist doll," I said. "My dad gave it to me as a gift."

I could see that Travis had begun to tremble. "That's it!" he cried. "That's him. Watch out. He can make you do things!"

Officer Marcus stood up and took Slappy from

me. I saw the dummy blink. But no one else seemed to notice.

The policeman held Slappy by the neck, and the dummy's arms and legs fell limply down. The officer shook Slappy hard. The arms and legs dangled loosely. He tilted the dummy's head back, then forward. Slappy's eyes stared blankly straight ahead.

Then Officer Marcus wrapped his hands around Slappy's shoes and held the dummy upside down. The dummy hung lifelessly from the officer's hands.

He turned to Travis. "No magic," he said. "Just a doll. He isn't alive." He shoved Slappy at Travis. "*You* take him."

"NO!" Travis threw his hands in the air.

Slappy fell to the floor. His head bounced once on the carpet. He didn't move.

Mr. Fox lifted Slappy up and handed him back to me. He shook his head. "Travis," he said, "when you feel like it, you can tell me what *really* happened."

"But—" Travis started to protest. He could see it was no use.

The three of them started to the door. I followed, cradling the dummy in my arms.

"Mr. Fox," the officer said, "perhaps Travis should see a doctor. Or maybe an *eye* doctor."

"So sorry to waste your time," Mr. Fox replied.

I pulled open the front door. Officer Marcus and Mr. Fox stepped onto the front stoop.

As soon as they were out of the house, Slappy lifted his head. He leaned out of my arms—and clamped his teeth hard on Travis's arm. I heard a *crunch* sound as Slappy bit harder.

"Owwwww!" Travis uttered a cry of pain.

Officer Marcus and Travis's dad spun around quickly. But by that time, Slappy's head slouched lifelessly in my arms. Far from Travis's arm.

"He bit me!" Travis cried, pointing at the dummy.

"Let's just go home," Mr. Fox said.

I closed the door after they left. Slappy sat up and slapped me a high five. "That was awesome!" he exclaimed. "Friends forever! Now let's see how we can mess with that guy Kelly!"

30

Kelly lived in an old brick house near the marshes on the other side of our school. His father worked at one of the casinos here in Atlantic City. His mother was a librarian at a high school.

Kelly and I had been pretty good friends. We hung out at each other's houses and played basketball in his backyard. We were friends until Travis came along in fourth grade. Then Kelly decided to be Travis's buddy—and my enemy!

Both of his parents were big readers, and the house was filled with books on tall bookshelves everywhere.

I guess that's why Kelly never read anything. Too many books to choose from. Ha.

I carried Slappy to Kelly's house in a big laundry bag. He wanted to walk. But no way was I letting that happen.

"Now don't go too far this time," I said. "We just want to scare Kelly. We don't want to hurt him or put him in danger."

"Maybe just a little?" Slappy said from inside the bag.

"No," I said. "We don't want to do anything that will bring the police to my house."

"Awwww." Slappy sighed. "What if Kelly just loses a little blood?"

"No blood," I said. "We just want to make Kelly promise not to be a beast and make my life miserable. Can you stick to that, Slappy?"

Silence for a long while. "What are friends for?" Slappy replied finally.

The laundry bag bounced over my shoulder as I walked. It was starting to feel heavy.

The afternoon sun had nearly set, but the air was still hot. I felt drops of sweat roll down my cheeks.

Kelly's house was half hidden behind a row of tall evergreen shrubs. The doors were open on the four-car garage in back. I saw two ancient black cars inside. Mr. Washington likes to tinker with old cars.

Groaning, I shifted the laundry bag to my other shoulder and walked up the long driveway to Kelly's house. The front door had a big stained-glass window in it. I pulled back the brass knocker and knocked really loudly.

"Remember," I whispered into the bag, "scare him, but not too much."

"You're talking to a master of scares, Barty, my friend," Slappy replied.

The door opened. Kelly blinked a few times, surprised. "You?"

I nodded. "Yeah. Me. Can I come in?"

"Why?" Kelly demanded. Not too friendly.

"Just want to talk," I said.

He backed up so I could enter the house. A bright chandelier stood overhead in the wide entryway. It took my eyes a few seconds to adjust to the light.

"You can't stay," Kelly said. "My mom will be right back. She is having a thing here in a few minutes."

I followed him through the living room. A big painting of his parents stood over the fireplace mantel. Two walls were covered with bookshelves.

"A thing?" I said. I still hadn't pulled Slappy from the laundry bag.

"She invited her book club to dinner," Kelly said.

We stopped at the entryway to the dining room. The long table was covered in a white tablecloth. White china plates, wine glasses, and silverware sparkled and gleamed at each setting. A huge centerpiece of red and yellow flowers was placed in the middle of the table.

"It looks awesome," I said, taking a few steps into the room. "Very fancy."

"Stay out of here," Kelly said, grabbing my shoulder. "Mom warned me not to touch a thing. She worked all morning on the table."

"I'd hate to see it messed up," I said.

Kelly's mouth formed a scowl. "What do you mean?" he snapped. "Are you trying to be funny, Sluggs?"

I shook my head. "No. I don't want to be funny."

"What *do* you want?" Kelly snarled. "Why are you here, Sluggs?"

"It's simple," I said. "I need you to swear that you'll be nice to me from now on."

Kelly squinted at me like I was some kind of alien from outer space. "Be nice to you?" he said. "Why would I be nice to you?"

"Because I'm asking you," I said. I saw Slappy squirming inside the laundry bag. I knew he was eager to get out.

Kelly gave me a push. "I'm asking you to get out of here, okay?"

"Is that a no?" I said. "You really shouldn't say no, Kelly. I'll show you why."

I raised the bottom of the laundry bag and spilled Slappy out onto the floor. The dummy's head and shoes clattered loudly on the wood floorboards.

Kelly stared down at it. "You brought your dummy? You're so weird, Sluggs."

"No, I'm not," I said. "I knew I'd need to convince you—"

Kelly laughed and grabbed my face. He squeezed my upper lip and my chin and made my mouth go up and down. *"Look at me. I'm a dummy!*" he said in a shrill voice. Then he laughed.

He stopped laughing when Slappy jumped to his feet.

"Hey—how'd you do that, Sluggs?" Kelly asked. "Never mind. Just take your stupid dummy and get out of here!" he shouted. His eyes were on the dining room window. "My mom just drove up the driveway."

"Promise you'll be nice to me from now on and I'll leave," I said.

"Just leave," Kelly shot back.

I heard the back door open. "I'm back!" Mrs. Washington called from the kitchen.

"Get out! I'm not promising anything!" Kelly said in a loud whisper. "Travis and I will teach you—"

"I don't think Travis will help you," I said. "Travis has changed his mind about me. I'm giving you one last chance."

Kelly shook his head. "Do I look stupid to you?"

"Well . . ."

"Do you like to dance?" Slappy interrupted.

Kelly's mouth dropped open. "How did you make the dummy talk?"

His mom walked into the dining room. Her eyes went wide when she saw me there. "Barton? Hi. How are you?"

"Fine," I said.

"You brought a puppet?" she said, staring at Slappy. "To show Kelly?"

"Kind of," I said.

"You boys had better get out of this room," she said. "I have all my most expensive china and glassware on the table. It took me hours to set the table."

"Okay," I said. "We'll get out."

"But first, Kelly wants to show you a new dance he learned," Slappy said.

Mrs. Washington turned her back to adjust a flower arrangement. She didn't realize the dummy had talked.

And she didn't see Slappy swing both hands toward Kelly, then move them high in the air.

Kelly made a gulping sound as he floated off the floor and drifted high over our heads. "Hey—!" A startled gasp escaped his throat. He thrashed his arms in the air. "What's happening?"

Slappy swept his hands to the side and Kelly moved through the air. Now he hovered over the dining room table . . . then settled down, down, down as Slappy lowered him. His shoes smashed a plate as he landed on the table.

The crash made Mrs. Washington spin around. She gaped at Kelly in horror. "Kelly! Get down! Get off the table! Have you lost your mind?"

Slappy crossed his hands in front of him and whispered a few words I couldn't hear.

And up on the tabletop, Kelly began to do a

dance. His shoes bounced up and down and his arms sailed out to his sides. And he began to tap-dance.

"Kelly! STOP!" his mother screamed. "STOP!"

Kelly's shoes beat out a fast tap rhythm. Plates and glasses shattered and went flying. He crushed wine glasses beneath his shoes and sent a long serving platter sailing toward the dining room window. It fell to the floor and cracked into a thousand pieces.

"Faster!" Slappy whispered. And Kelly, helpless to stop himself, danced even faster over the table.

Mrs. Washington screamed and tore at her hair. She made a grab for Kelly. But he backed out of her reach and kept up his wild tap dance.

He kicked the centerpiece and began to dance on top of it. Flowers and dirt flew off the table.

"Stop! STOP!" Mrs. Washington shrieked. "What are you DOING? STOP!"

Finally, Kelly turned to me and cried out breathlessly. "Okay! I promise! I'll never be mean to you again! Just let me stop! Please!"

Slappy twirled his hands together. Kelly did a high backflip off the table and landed on the floor on his feet. He blinked, stunned, his eyes rolling in his head.

Mrs. Washington grabbed him by the shoulders. "Kelly! Why? Why?" she screamed. "You ruined everything. Look at this mess. Everything is broken. Glass everywhere! Have you lost your mind?"

Kelly didn't answer.

I quickly shoved Slappy back into the laundry bag.

"Sorry, Mrs. Washington," I said. "I hope this wasn't my fault."

She squinted at me. "Your fault? How *could* it be your fault, Barton? Kelly went berserk. It couldn't be your fault."

"Well, I'm sorry," I repeated. "I hope Kelly is okay."

I heard him mutter something under his breath. But I didn't wait to hear what he said. I slung the laundry bag over my shoulder and hurried out of the house.

I didn't breathe until I was down the long driveway and back to the street.

Inside the bag, Slappy laughed. "That was awesome! You didn't know Kelly had so much talent, did you, Barty?"

"I never saw him dance before," I replied. "He was pretty good."

"And he promised he'd never try to bully you again, my friend," Slappy said. "Slappy to the rescue."

"Yeah. Thanks," I said. I was picturing the mess we left behind. Broken china and glass all over the room. I felt sorry for Kelly's mom. It would take her hours to clean up.

"Well, my friend, this is fun," Slappy said, bouncing in the laundry bag as we walked. "Who's next?"

"Next?" I said. "No, you're confused. I told you, Slappy. No one is next."

"That girl. Lizzie," he said. "She's next."

"No. Wait, Slappy—" I protested.

"She's next!" he cried. "She can't be your friend. Because *I'm* your friend. We'll teach her a lesson!"

"No. Wait." I stopped.

Slappy lowered his voice to a nasty rasp. "Let's go get her," he said. "Walk!"

32

I crossed the street. My brain was buzzing. I couldn't let Slappy hurt Lizzie. I should have known he would take the friend thing too far.

Lizzie was my only true friend in the world. And now the evil dummy thought he would help me by teaching her a frightening lesson.

I knew it was time to stop him. But how?

I turned back to the street. I saw three large SUVs rolling toward me.

I suddenly knew what I had to do.

I reached into the bag and pulled Slappy halfway out. "Are we there?" he rasped. "Are we at that girl Lizzie's house?"

"Not quite," I said.

I wrapped both hands around the dummy's head.

"You don't have to hug me," he said. "I know I'm your best friend."

With a desperate, hard tug, I pulled Slappy's head off—

—and tossed it through the back window of a passing SUV.

Yes, I imagined that.

If only I could act that bravely in real life.

I didn't tear off Slappy's head and toss it away. It seemed like such a good plan. And it worked so well in my mind.

But what would Slappy *really* do if I made a grab for his head? I didn't want to find out.

So before I knew it, I was at Lizzie's house. "She is up in her room," her mom said. "But you can't stay long. We're going to a cousin's for dinner."

"It won't take long," Slappy said inside the bag.

Mrs. Hellman squinted at me. "Do you have a cold, Barton? Your voice sounds funny."

"No. I'm fine," I said. I turned and walked down the long hall to Lizzie's room.

She was on her knees on the floor, surrounded by dozens of stuffed dogs. She looked up as I stepped into the room.

"I can't decide which ones to use for my project," she said. "Maybe you can help me."

"Help you?" I said. I could see Slappy squirming to get out of the bag.

"Well, my topic is the history of dogs as pets. So I need to show some ancient-looking dogs. Or maybe early breeds that people first adopted."

She fumbled through a big pile of stuffed animals. "Here. Like this one." She held up what looked like a creature that was part German shepherd, part wolf. "The first dogs that people tamed were descended from wolves."

"That's a good one," I said.

Lizzie turned her gaze to the laundry bag. "Barton, what's in there?"

"It . . . it's Slappy!" I cried. My voice was suddenly choked with panic. "We have to do something, Lizzie. Get up! Get up! We have to run! He's out of control!"

"What do you mean?" she cried.

Before I could answer, Slappy squirmed out of the bag and jumped to his feet. He poked his hand angrily at Lizzie. "You can't be Barton's friend!" he exclaimed. "I am Barton's friend. His *only* friend!"

I tried to grab the dummy. But he slid out of my grasp and backed to the wall. "Leave Lizzie alone!" I begged. "Please—Slappy. Lizzie can be my friend, too."

"No way!" he rasped. "I am your only friend. Your *best* friend forever. This girl Lizzie has to go. Good-bye, Lizzie!"

33

Lizzie jumped to her feet. She still had the stuffed German shepherd in her hand. She tossed it at Slappy, and it bounced off his head. "Leave us alone!" she cried.

"You shouldn't have done that," the dummy growled.

He swept a hand in front of his chest, and the bedroom door slammed shut.

Lizzie darted to the door. She turned the knob and pulled. "We're locked in!"

Slappy tossed back his head and laughed. "Cozy, isn't it?"

I dove at him. Tried to tackle him to the floor. But he slipped out of my hands and leaped onto the bed.

"Lizzie the Dog Lover!" he screamed. "Let's see how much you love your dogs!"

"Slappy, don't—!" I cried. I lurched toward the bed. But I tripped over some stuffed dogs and stumbled to the floor.

Slappy raised both hands high above his head and shouted out some strange words.

And as I struggled to my feet, I saw the stuffed dogs begin to change. The little dogs were growing taller, wider. And their cute faces were changing. Pointed fangs curled down from their mouths.

"Noooo! Stop!" Lizzie cried. She tried the door again. It wouldn't budge.

I made another grab for Slappy. Giggling, he dodged away.

The stuffed dogs stretched and grew. Dozens of them. Standing as tall as HORSES now. Horse-sized dogs with monster faces. Growing . . . stretching . . .

Lizzie and I backed against the wall. The enormous stuffed creatures were filling the room now. No room for us to move. And still they kept swelling up.

And then: POPPPPPPPPPP!

A cloud of white fuzz exploded into the air.

POPPP POPPP.

The giant stuffed dogs were exploding!

The explosions blasted Lizzie and me to the floor. I hit my back hard, and my breath whooshed out.

Standing on the bed, Slappy opened his mouth in a cackling laugh.

POP POPPP.

Clumps of stuffing, thicker than snow, heavy, ragged, came plunging down on us.

"I can't see!" I cried.

"Can't breathe . . ." Lizzie moaned. "It . . . it's like a *blizzard*!"

POPPPP.

I shut my eyes as stuffing exploded into my face.

I started to choke. I grabbed Lizzie. She was choking, too. I struggled to see, to breathe.

And over the explosions of stuffing, the only sound was the laughter of the evil dummy.

34

Lizzie struggled to her feet. The clumps of stuffing came up to her knees. She grabbed my hand and pulled me up. Then she pounded on the bedroom door with both fists. "Mom! Mom—help us!"

Slappy laughed. "She'll never hear you."

I pulled chunks of stuffing from my hair. I wiped my face with both hands. Choking and coughing, I pulled stuffing from my nose and mouth.

I stood there, gazing at the mess. The floor looked like a stuffed dog graveyard, with torn animals scattered everywhere, half-buried in white and yellow stuffing.

"Lizzie—do you get my message?" Slappy screamed from the bed. "My message is simple: Stay away from my friend Barton. Do you get it?"

Still gripping the doorknob, Lizzie stared back at him and didn't reply.

"Keep him talking," I whispered. "I have an idea."

She nodded and turned to the dummy. "Why can't you be *my* friend?" she demanded.

"Because I'm Barton's friend," Slappy replied. "Barton was the first kid who ever *liked* me. The first kid who wasn't scared of me."

"So now you can only be Barton's friend?" Lizzie said.

Slappy's grin appeared to grow wider. "You got that right, sister. You know what that means? That means *you* get lost."

As they talked, I slid along the wall, moving closer to Slappy. He stood at the edge of Lizzie's bed, waving his hands in the air as he shouted at her.

I took one step. Then another. My eyes were on Slappy's suit jacket. I saw something in the jacket pocket that gave me a good idea.

An idea for stopping the evil dummy. An idea for getting him out of my life.

It was a little slip of white in his jacket pocket. And I remembered. The sheet of paper with the strange words. The words that had brought Slappy to life.

What would happen if I read those words again?

Would they put him back to sleep?

It was a wild, desperate idea. But I didn't have any others. I had no choice. I had to try it.

Slappy and Lizzie kept up their argument. Lizzie was watching me as I crept closer to the screaming dummy. Closer.

When I was close enough, I threw myself at Slappy. I tackled him around the legs and brought him down on his back.

He uttered an angry cry and tried to bat me with his fists.

But I ducked under them and grabbed the front of his jacket.

"What are you doing?" the dummy cried. "We're friends! Are you forgetting that we're friends for life?"

I ignored his screams and dug my fingers into his jacket pocket.

Yes!

I pulled the sheet of paper from the pocket.

I raised it high and unfolded it.

Would this work? If I shouted the weird words, would they put Slappy to sleep?

The paper trembled in my hand. I started to raise it close enough to read . . .

. . . and Slappy grabbed it away from me!

"Give that back!" I cried. I swiped at it. Missed.

The dummy giggled. And stuffed the paper into his mouth.

"Noooo!" I let out a horrified cry.

And watched him chew the paper to bits and swallow it.

35

He made a *gulp* sound as he swallowed the last chunk of paper. Then he burped and grinned at me. "Friends for life, Barty, my boy." He tossed back his head and laughed. The shrill sound bounced off the walls and ceiling.

I covered my ears.

My chest heaved with every breath. I stared at him, helpless. Was that my one chance to defeat him? My only chance?

Maybe not.

I blinked as a thought flashed into my mind.

"You know what, my friend?" Slappy said. "I know something better than friendship. From now on, you won't just be my friend. You'll be my *servant*! Hahaha!"

"I don't think so," I said. And I grabbed him again. I wrapped my arms around his waist and dropped him onto his back.

My fingers fumbled in the jacket pocket until

I found what I was looking for. "OKAY!" I screamed. "Okay! Okay!"

I tugged the sheet of paper from the pocket.

I remembered there were *two* sheets folded up and tucked in the pocket. Not one piece of paper—*two* pieces of paper!

Again, my hands shook as I unfolded it. And stared at the strange secret words. Yes! This was the right one!

I couldn't stop myself. I laughed. "You ate the *wrong sheet of paper, Slappy!*" I shouted.

He ate the one that said *Hi. My name is Slappy. Do you want to be my friend?*

"Give me that!" he screamed.

He tried to jump up. But I kept him pinned to the bed. And I shouted the words as loudly as I could:

"KARRU MARRI ODONNA LOMA MOLONU KARRANO."

Would it put the evil dummy to sleep?

"Sorry," Slappy said. "That doesn't work."

"That doesn't work," Slappy said. "I . . . I . . ."

He collapsed and slumped onto his back. His eyelids slid down over his eyes. His mouth shut tight with a loud wooden *click*. His arms and legs went limp.

Lizzie stepped up beside me. We both stared at him without speaking, waiting for him to sit up, to open his eyes . . . to move.

But he didn't.

"It worked!" I cried. "He's totally asleep."

Lizzie let out a long sigh. "Wow. I mean, wow. Thank goodness."

"Yeah. He wasn't a very good friend," I said.

Lizzie frowned at me. "Do you think?"

She leaned over the dummy, as if making sure he really was out cold. "What are you going to do now?"

"Lock him back in his case," I said. "And dump the case as far away as I can. I'll take a bus to the beach and—"

"Oh my goodness!" a voice interrupted.

We both spun around. Lizzie's mom poked her head into the room. Her mouth dropped open as she stared at the ripped and shredded animals and heaps of stuffing that covered the room.

"Wh-what on earth happened in here?" she cried.

"Oh, I was just rearranging my collection," Lizzie said.

It took a long time to clean up. We were at it for a few days. When we were finally done, we decided to go for a walk, just to clear our minds and calm down. It's hard to calm down when you've been living in a horror movie!

It was a warm, sunny afternoon. Everything seemed to sparkle brightly. Maybe it was just my mood. Maybe everything looked magical because I was so happy.

We walked around the soccer field at school. Travis and Kelly were watching a game from the sidelines. I waved to them.

They hesitated for a moment, then waved back.

My new best friends!

"Let's go to my house," I said to Lizzie. "We can pick up Slappy and get rid of him."

"The sooner the better," Lizzie agreed.

We were half a block from my house when we heard the growls. The growls quickly became deafening barks and howls.

"Kraken!" I cried.

The huge dog came charging at us, big paws pounding the ground. His head was lowered. His eyes shone like yellow headlights.

Was the chain attached?

I couldn't see.

I grabbed Lizzie's arm, and we stood there frozen in panic.

Kraken came to a lumbering stop, just inches from us. He raised his big head and pulled back his ears. And the dog said, *"Hey, Barty, don't you want to be my friend?"*

Or did I just imagine that?

EPILOGUE FROM SLAPPY

That kid Barton has a great imagination. Do you believe it? He *imagined* he could defeat me! Hahaha!

I imagine I'll wake up in time to star in another book. I always do.

Barton was a good friend. But he didn't understand the First Rule of Friendship: *Do it to others before they do it to you!* Hahahaha.

Well, time for me to go, my friend. But don't feel bad. I'll be back soon with another Goosebumps story.

Remember, this is *SlappyWorld.*

You only *scream* in it!

SLAPPYWORLD #13: MONSTER BLOOD IS BACK

Read on for a preview!

1

On the day my friend Nicole and I found the Monster Blood and totally ruined our lives, we were both excited and happy enough to burst.

That's because we had a chance to be on our favorite TV series.

A chance to show off the cooking skills we had practiced in my kitchen. All the crazy dishes Nicole and I dreamed up. Slapping food together in the craziest combinations. Dreaming up wild new desserts and pasta casseroles and soups and stews that sometimes even *we* were afraid to taste!

Before I go too far, let me say that I'm Sascha Nelson. My best friend Nicole Miller and I are twelve, and we consider ourselves kitchen explorers. *We go where no chefs have ever gone before.*

No joke.

I mean, who else would think of making salty chocolate milk? Or scrambled eggs with marshmallow fluff? Or a bologna cake?

We're pioneers. We're inventors. We're creators. We're totally nuts.

At least, that's what my mom and dad say. But what do *they* know? They put jelly on their peanut butter instead of bananas and pickles!

Who could compete against us in the kitchen?

We were about to find out. Because—wait for this— Nicole and I were picked for the most awesome TV cooking show in the universe.

Unless you're new to this planet, you know what I'm talking about. *Kids' Big Chef Food Fights.*

That's the one. Three teams of kids competing for the Silver Spatula. That spatula is worth $2,000!

Can you get excited about $2,000? Nicole and I sure could.

All of the contestants were coming from our school, Adam Driver Middle School. Nicole and I knew we could outcook anyone in school with our oven mitts tied behind our back.

Sure. Maybe I brag a lot. But if you've got something to brag about, why not?

After school on Friday, we couldn't wait to get to the TV studio. Luckily, it was only a six-block walk from my house. Nicole and I were in my kitchen, loosening up.

"Let's make an ice cream sundae," I said. "Put everything we can find on it."

Nicole nodded. "Yeah. We need to carb up,

you know." She flexed her arm muscles. "Get the energy flowing."

"Mainly I just want a sundae," I said.

We pulled a carton of vanilla ice cream from the freezer. I found chopped walnuts and caramel syrup and colored sprinkles in the pantry. Nicole produced a banana from the fridge. "Do you have any popcorn?" she asked. "I love popcorn on ice cream."

"I don't think so," I said. "There's a bag of tortilla chips. We could crumble some chips on it."

I found a tall can of fake whipped cream in the refrigerator door. You know, the whipped cream with a nozzle that you push and it sprays out.

"This is a good start," I said. "We can build the sundae, then see what else we can find."

Nicole glanced at the clock above the kitchen window. "It's getting late. Maybe we should just have some ice cream."

"No way," I insisted. "This is going to be an awesome creation."

I pulled a glass ice cream dish from the cabinet and started to scoop ice cream into it. Nicole heated the caramel sauce in the microwave. Then she poured it on top of the ice cream scoops.

We were adding the banana slices when Toby came bursting into the kitchen.

Toby is my little brother. He's eight going on four. What I mean is, he's a pain.

About the Author

R.L. Stine says he gets to scare people all over the world. So far, his books have sold more than 400 million copies, making him one of the most popular children's authors in history. The Goosebumps series has more than 150 titles and has inspired a TV series and two motion pictures. R.L. himself is a character in the movies! He has also written the teen series Fear Street, and the Mostly Ghostly and Nightmare Room series. He is currently writing a series of graphic novels entitled Just Beyond. R.L. Stine lives in New York City with his wife, Jane, an editor and publisher. You can learn more about him at rlstine.com.

The Original Bone-Chilling Series
Goosebumps®
—with Exclusive Author Interviews!
NIGHT of the LIVING DUMMY
DEEP TROUBLE
MONSTER BLOOD
The HAUNTED MASK
ONE DAY at HORRORLAND
the CURSE of the MUMMY'S TOMB
BE CAREFUL WHAT YOU WISH FOR
SAY CHEESE and DIE!
the HORROR at CAMP JELLYJAM
HOW I GOT MY SHRUNKEN HEAD
R.L. STINE
SCHOLASTIC
SCHOLASTIC and associated logos are trademarks and/or registered trademarks of Scholastic Inc.
www.scholastic.com/goosebumps
GBCL22

R. L. Stine's Fright Fest!
Now with Splat Stats and More!
Goosebumps
The Werewolf of Fever Swamp
R.L. Stine
Goosebumps
A Night in Terror Tower
R.L. Stine
Goosebumps
Welcome to Dead House
R.L. Stine
Goosebumps
Welcome to Camp Nightmare
R.L. Stine
Goosebumps
Ghost Beach
R.L. Stine
Goosebumps
The Scarecrow Walks at Midnight
R.L. Stine
Goosebumps
You Can't Scare Me!
R.L. Stine
Goosebumps
Return of the Mummy
R.L. Stine
Goosebumps
Revenge of the Lawn Gnomes
R.L. Stine
Goosebumps
Phantom of the Auditorium
R.L. Stine
Goosebumps
Vampire Breath
R.L. Stine
Goosebumps
Stay Out of the Basement
R.L. Stine
SCHOLASTIC
Read them all!

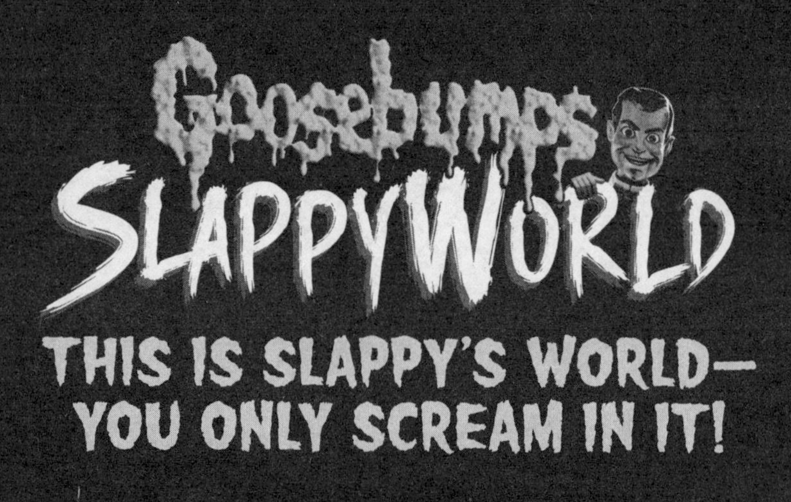
Goosebumps
SlappyWorld
THIS IS SLAPPY'S WORLD—
YOU ONLY SCREAM IN IT!

SLAPPY BIRTHDAY TO YOU
R.L. STINE
ATTACK OF THE JACK!
R.L. STINE
I AM SLAPPY'S EVIL TWIN
R.L. STINE
PLEASE DO NOT FEED THE WEIRDO
R.L. STINE
ESCAPE FROM SHUDDER MANSION
R.L. STINE
THE GHOST OF SLAPPY
R.L. STINE
IT'S ALIVE! IT'S ALIVE!
R.L. STINE
THE DUMMY MEETS THE MUMMY!
R.L. STINE
REVENGE OF THE INVISIBLE BOY!
R.L. STINE
DIARY OF A DUMMY
R.L. STINE
THEY CALL ME THE NIGHT HOWLER!
R.L. STINE
MY FRIEND SLAPPY
R.L. STINE
MONSTER BLOOD IS BACK
R.L. STINE
SCHOLASTIC
GBSLAPPYWORLD12